Todd came up behind her and wrapped his arms around her

"That was nice of you, babe, but never thank me for telling the truth. You can feed me," he added pointedly. "Especially if you plan on taking advantage of me again." He let go of her just enough to move her hair out of the way so he could kiss her neck, which he did with great skill and desire.

"You'd better stop that if you plan to eat, because I can assure you I have plans for you," she said in a sultry voice.

He turned her around so they were facing each other and he pressed the lower part of his body into hers. "On second thought, I can wait a little while longer for food, but I still need to eat. Have you ever made love in a kitchen?"

Books by Melanie Schuster

Kimani Romance

Working Man
Model Perfect Passion
Trust in Me
A Case for Romance
Picture Perfect Christmas
Chemistry of Desire

MELANIE SCHUSTER

attributes her love of writing to her love of reading. She was lucky enough to be born to parents who were avid readers and she learned to read before she started school. She is still a voracious reader of all genres, that is, when she's not on deadline! When she's not writing, she enjoys painting, shopping online for rare books, making jewelry and sewing. She also loves to cook, and is working on a very special cookbook based on her novels. She lives in Michigan with her very sassy and slightly spoiled dog, Sadie.

Chemistry
of
Desire

Melanie
Schuster

KIMANI
ROMANCE

Dedicated with love to Evette Porter
and ShaShana Crichton. Thanks for everything, always.

 KIMANI PRESS™

ISBN-13: 978-0-373-86223-8

Recycling programs
for this product may
not exist in your area.

CHEMISTRY OF DESIRE

www.kimanipress.com

Printed in U.S.A.

Dear Reader,

For all of you who wanted to know more about the delectable Todd Wainwright from *Model Perfect Passion,* this one's for you! And it will also answer any questions you had about Ayanna's grumpy sister, Emily, from *A Case for Romance.* Emily was a grouchy, antisocial workaholic who got a whole new outlook on life, as well as a new appearance, thanks to her BFFs. But it might have been a bit too much of a change for a man who already thought she was perfect from head to toe. He was already attracted to her, but the new version scared him off. Love and understanding, along with communication, conquer all for this seemingly mismatched couple.

Thank you all for the prayers and love you've been sending my way. I love and appreciate all of you more than I can say.

Stay blessed!

Melanie

I *Chronicles* 4:10

Many thanks and much love to my ride-or-die readers
and friends. Thanks for believing in me
and supporting me every step of the way.
A special thanks to Betty, Louise, Kimmi-Kim, Nicole,
Patsy, Pam and "Miss Begina". No one can do it all
without a support system and
you ladies make my hard road much easier.
Love you all!

Prologue

The hallway of the middle school was quiet, much quieter than it was during the normal school day. There were only a few students left taking part in after-school activities. Two girls were lingering outside the gym, eavesdropping for all they were worth. One was tall and rail thin, and the other was so short she could have been in elementary school. They were standing as still as possible and listening to every word being spoken in the gym, which wasn't hard because the words echoed loudly in the corridor due to the poor soundproofing.

The first voice was the coach of the girls dance team, Mrs. Carter. "Emily, you need to find another after-school activity. You're just not suited for dance."

A second voice chimed in. This time it was the assistant coach, Mrs. Johnson. "You just don't have the feminine grace to succeed in dance. You would do better in soccer or basketball, something like that."

"I don't understand," Emily said, her voice clear but slightly shaky. "I can do all the dances and I don't forget the steps. I know all of the moves we're supposed to do, so why can't I dance?"

"Just because you *can* do something doesn't mean you *should*," Mrs. Carter said condescendingly. "I'm sure you thought you could do this because your older sisters were such lovely dancers, but this just isn't for you."

"But I can do it," Emily protested. "I can show you."

Mrs. Johnson cut in. "We're not trying to hurt your feelings, but our decision is final. Get your things and get on home. Think about something else you'd like to participate in, because you're not getting on the dance squad. You are so different from your sisters, it's like night and day. They're so petite and graceful, and you're just not. Face it, dear—you're just too big and clumsy-looking for this. Find another activity."

The two girls looked at each other with anger and indignation. Emily was their best friend, and nobody had the right to be so mean to her. They heard the door to the locker room forced open as Emily went to get her things. They also heard the two women continue to talk to each other.

"I don't know how that girl could be related to Attiya and Ayanna. They got all the beauty in that family, and that's the truth," said Mrs. Carter.

"They took after their mother," Mrs. Johnson agreed. "That Emily looks like a big ol' bear next to them. It's a good thing she gets good grades, because she has nothing else going for her. It must be hard being the big ugly one in a pretty family."

"Too bad for her," Mrs. Carter agreed. "Turn off the lights and let's get out of here."

The two girls waited until the lights went out in the gym before running into the locker room to get their friend. The teachers left by the side entrance and didn't even notice that Emily was still in the locker room. The girls got there just in time to see Emily wiping away angry tears.

"I'm not going out for the dance team," she mumbled. "I'm not going out for anything. I'm going home."

"Don't listen to those old bats," said the short one, who was named Alexis. "They're just old and senile, and they don't know what they're talking about."

The tall one, named Sherri, agreed. "You should tell your mother and get them suspended without pay, because they have no right to say those things to a student. It's discriminatory."

They were trying to make her feel better, but it didn't really work. She'd been hearing the same kind of things from people since she was a little girl. Nothing she ever did was good enough, because she didn't look like her sisters. It wasn't her fault that she was tall and sturdy instead of little and gorgeous. So she was done trying to be like them. From now on she was going to be the smartest girl in the family, since she couldn't be anything else. And she had something else to look forward to, according to Sherri.

"Don't worry about it, because tomorrow I'ma put a worm in their desks. That'll fix the old hags."

Emily was surprised that she could laugh, but she did. They all laughed together as they left the building and started the long walk home.

Chapter 1

"Do you think she'll cuss us out?" Alexis sounded more amused than nervous as she checked the contents of her shopping bag.

"Probably. But she needs to vent to somebody or she'll pop. It's our duty to annoy her enough to let it out." Sherri was always practical, down-to-earth and fearless. And she would probably need all of those characteristics to deal with their BFF today. She turned off the ignition and reached into the backseat to get the bag she'd brought. She turned to Alexis with a face of determination. "Let's get it over with. Emily's had her panties in a knot for weeks, and it's past time that we find out why. Get out of the car."

Alexis frowned. "If she wanted us to know what's been bothering her, she'd have told us. She's entitled to her privacy," she pointed out.

"Get out of the car. She doesn't need privacy, she needs her girls. Out!"

They finally made it to the green front door of the cottage. It was a perfect little jewel of a house. Emily had done almost all the renovation work herself, and the results were spectacular. Alexis looked ready to bolt, but Sherri grabbed her arm with one hand while she rang the bell with the other. "Girl, if you make me drop this bottle of wine, I will hurt you," she threatened.

Luckily, Emily answered the door before mayhem could ensue. She had been exercising from the looks of her; she was wearing workout clothes that bore large sweat patterns around the neck and the armpits, and she was wiping more sweat from her face. "What a surprise," she said dryly. "So what is this, an intervention?"

Sherri sucked her teeth. "Yes, it is. And it wouldn't be necessary if you would just confide in your best friends like a normal woman. Move out of the way so we can come in before we drop this stuff."

Emily didn't budge. "What stuff? Is it edible?"

Alexis nodded vigorously. "We brought you dinner, and it's hella good." Emily moved out of the doorway so they could enter the house. As

Alexis walked past her, she whispered, "Sherri made me ambush you. This was all her idea."

Sadly, Alexis had never really learned how to whisper, so Sherri heard every word. "I'll get you later. In the meantime, let's eat," Sherri said cheerfully. "We'll set the table while you go shower, Miss Emily."

"Fine, if you're gonna gang up on me," Emily mumbled, but she really didn't sound angry. She actually sounded a little relieved, but only someone who knew her very well would have noticed.

In a short time the ladies were sitting at the table in the breakfast room off Emily's kitchen. It was spotless, as was every room of the house. The walls were pale green, matching the green-and-white ceramic tile floor. All the trim was black, matching the black and stainless steel appliances and the black table and chairs. The chairs had seats covered in green-and-white-patterned fabric that matched the café curtains in the windows that surrounded the seating area.

"What are we eating?" Emily asked. "Not that I care, of course. You know I'll eat anything."

"I brought some chicken salad and rolls and brownies," Alexis told her.

"Brought out the big guns, huh? You're really trying to make me talk, aren't you?" Emily put a big helping of salad on her plate and took two of the crusty homemade rolls. Alexis made astounding chicken salad, and Emily could never get enough of it.

Sherri poured her a glass of pinot grigio. "Yes, this is a bribe. It's come to that, Em. You've been acting like a different person since you took that trip to Hilton Head in September and we want to know why. You have been avoiding us, and when we do manage to get in touch with you, you're in a nasty-ass mood, the one that scares most people off. We've been friends since grade school, and you can't scare us off," she said. "But there has to be a good explanation for your errant behavior, and we want to know what it is. Time for you to share, sister."

Emily looked at Sherri and then at Alexis. The three of them had been friends forever. They were really the only people she was close to, outside of her family. All of them were pretty, but they couldn't have been more dissimilar. Emily was tall and bronze, with long, thick black hair that she never did anything to, other than keep it clean. She was in perfect shape, thanks to years of yoga, cycling and karate. Nothing fussy or girlish about her, but she was a very busy woman. Head of the biochemistry department at University of South Carolina, her schedule was loaded with academics as well as community service. She had too much on her plate to mess around with cosmetics—at least that was her excuse.

Alexis, on the other hand, was petite with chocolate-brown skin, and her hair was always chic. Since she was a much sought-after cosmetologist, her hair was her advertisement; it had better be fly. Sherri was even taller than Emily and very striking. She was very fair-skinned with short red hair, and she was always fashionably attired even though she was as busy as Emily, if not busier. She was a doctor with a practice in family medicine, and she was also a single mother. But she would still take the time to put on a little makeup and some jewelry, two things that Emily ignored. Despite their differences in appearance and demeanor, they were truly close and always would be. When good things happened to them they celebrated, and when bad things happened they commiserated. What they didn't do was hold out on each other the way Emily was doing.

"You know we're not just being nosy," Alexis said. "Well, Sherri is, you know what a busybody she is. I'm truly concerned about you, sweetie." Her pious tone ended in a shriek as Sherri pinched her arm.

Emily was considerably mellower after her delicious dinner. "Look, if it's gonna keep you two from maiming each other, I will tell you why I've been in such a pissy mood for the last month. As

you already know, I went to Hilton Head the week
after my summer science camp. But what you don't
know is I had some company while I was there."

"Who?" Alexis and Sherri spoke in unison with
wide eyes.

"This will go faster if you don't interrupt. And
might I add you look like owls when you do that?
Okay, so this is what happened," she drawled.

Chapter 2

September
Hilton Head Island

It was a perfect fall day. The SUV was humming along the road, the sky was cloudless and blue and the music was blasting from the speakers. Todd Wainwright was feeling more relaxed than he had in months. When he saw the bright blue mailbox that was his landmark, he turned into the driveway. It was a long driveway that went up a slight incline, and there was a big barnlike garage at the end. He chose not to explore the garage, stopping instead next to the house, where he turned off the ignition and tried to stretch. The drive from Chicago had taken hours, and his long limbs were feeling the strain. He got out of the Expedition so he could get the kinks out of his body and take a look around at the same time.

The house was everything he was told it would be. It was beautiful, spacious, secluded and near the water. The house sat far back from the road and was surrounded by trees, mostly pine. He removed his sunglasses and took in a deep breath of the enticing scent of the sea and the fragrant scent of evergreen. For once he had listened to his friends and family back in Illinois, and he was glad he had. It was his brother's idea that he take some time off. It was his sister-in-law's notion that he needed to go out of town and his friend Ayanna had given him the keys to her family's vacation home on Hilton Head Island.

"You'll love it down there," she'd assured him. "Daddy was an architect and he not only designed the house, he built it himself. It's right on the beach, and it's kinda secluded so you'll get some rest and relaxation. My mother is in Africa right now and my sister Emily is off with her youth camp, so you can run around naked all day if you want to," she had teased him.

Todd had laughed and said he might just do that. Now, as he looked at the greenery surrounding the modern but rustic-looking home that awaited him, he grinned. Maybe running around without clothes was a possibility. The stitches were out and there was no reason to stay covered up anymore. Besides, Ayanna had said something about an outdoor hot tub that had sounded pretty good. He didn't bother to get his bags. He decided to take a look around and get his bearings first.

The exterior had a porch that extended around three sides. In the back there was a deck with a broad overhang that protected the hot tub Ayanna had mentioned. Todd had mounted the stairs and was standing on the deck when he realized the back door was open. The screen door was closed and locked, but the wood-and-glass door that opened into the kitchen was wide open. He sorted through the keys on the ring he was holding and found one that was labeled for the kitchen screen door. He opened the door and stepped into the kitchen, announcing himself so that he didn't scare whoever was in the house.

"This is Todd Wainwright, a friend of the family. I'm invited to use the house so I have keys," he said in his low, mellow voice.

He didn't get an answer, so he kept moving through the downstairs, looking into the great room that adjoined the kitchen, the living room and the media room. The house was even better on the inside. Everything was paneled in gleaming oak. The living room had a cathedral ceiling, and all the rooms had black ceiling fans that looked elegant instead of kitschy. The furnishings were simple and casual, yet the rooms exuded a touch of elegance. It looked like a layout from a *House Beautiful* magazine, but lived-in.

Todd kept walking around, repeating his original statement a couple of times but still getting no answer. He was at the foot of the stairs when he thought he heard something. Climbing the stairs to the second story, he continued to try to alert anyone who might be in the house. "I'm not a burglar, I'm not a pervert, and I was invited here by Ayanna. I got in with the keys she gave me," he said in a soothing voice, or what he hoped was soothing. He heard water splashing and followed the noise to what appeared to be a bathroom. The door was open, and the warm moisture in the room was heavy with the scent of flowers. And standing in the bathtub covered with creamy foam was Ayanna's sister Emily—naked as the day she was born, singing at the top of her lungs as she swayed under the spray of a handheld shower.

Todd's heart leaped to his throat and stayed there, lodged right next to his Adam's apple. He wanted to say something to let her know he was there, but he couldn't get a word out. He'd met Emily on a few occasions, but he couldn't currently make sense of what he was currently staring at. Her golden-brown skin gleamed with the droplets of water cascading over it. She had an amazing body, now that he could see it without clothes. Her back was to him, and he could see the perfect globes of her behind, her firm thighs and her long, curvy legs. Her long hair was full of shampoo, and she was using the shower attachment as a microphone. He'd never heard a version of "Single Ladies" as off-key and tuneless as the one Emily was wailing, but her beauty more than made up for it. Todd knew he had to get out of there fast or things would get real ugly.

He backed out of the doorway and silently made his way back downstairs. *Damn, that was close.* He couldn't have explained his actions in any way that would have made sense. He knew that Emily would've been angry and embarrassed about being spied on. And she'd have been completely justified, too. He knew better than to sneak up on a woman like that, even if it was an accident. Once she dried off and dressed, he could explain everything to her. In the meantime, he decided to sit on the porch and enjoy the breeze for a few minutes. He took a seat in one of oversize chairs with comfortable, thickly padded seat covers and propped his legs on a matching ottoman. He fell asleep almost at once, lulled by the soft wind and the chirping of the birds in the trees. He would have stayed that way for a long time, but a strange voice made his eyes pop open.

"Sir, do you care to explain why you're here?"

The first thing Todd focused on was a tall South Carolina state trooper who was watching him intently while he repeated his question. "Sir, I asked you why you were here."

Now that he was aware that the man's partner was also present, Todd answered him. "I was invited to stay here by the owner of this house."

"Well now, that's a funny thing. The owner of the house is the person who called us and reported a B&E. She doesn't seem to know you."

"There's been a big misunderstanding. I'm a friend of Ayanna Walker, uh, her married name is Phillips now. Anyway, she gave me the keys to the house and said no one would be here. But her sister Emily is home, and I was just waiting for her to come downstairs so I could let her know I was here." His words sounded bungled and inane even to him, but he figured it was better to tell the truth.

"Okay, sir, that sounds plausible, except for the part about your being a friend of the family, because Ms. Emily is the one who called us and she claims to not know you."

Just then a female head popped out of the door. Emily was fully clothed with her still-soapy hair draped over her shoulders in long tight ringlets. Her long-lashed eyes peered at him with suspicion. "Todd, is that you? When did you cut your hair?"

* * *

In a short time all the misunderstandings were ironed out and the troopers left, although the younger man was still giving Todd the side eye. Emily had felt totally foolish when she realized that it was indeed Todd and not some random stranger who had invaded her home. She had thrown on clothes hastily as she was calling 911 and was now attired in faded denim shorts with frayed edges and an equally faded T-shirt, complete with holes from years of wear. Her feet were bare and she should have looked like a typical tomboy, but she didn't. She looked quite sexy, as a matter of fact, but she wouldn't have believed it for a minute. Emily was much too down-to-earth to categorize herself as any kind of femme fatale.

"Well, come on in," she said. "You want some lemonade or sweet tea?"

"Sure."

They went into the kitchen and she poured him a glass of lemonade, offering him some fat sugar cookies to go with it.

"I'm really sorry," Todd said again. "I had no idea you were here, or I wouldn't have come. In fact, if you tell me where there's a hotel, I'll get out of your hair."

Emily ignored his comment and looked at him intently. "Speaking of hair, you never said why you cut yours," she pointed out.

Todd ran his hand over his head, which was shorn down to his scalp. The last time she'd seen him, he'd had long braids that came way past his shoulders. Now he was almost bald with a shadow beard and moustache.

"I cut it because I met a patient who was starting chemo. She came into the emergency room during a crisis, and I treated her before she was admitted. Cutest little girl you ever saw," he added. "Anyway, she knew she was going to lose all her hair, so I told her I'd shave my head so we'd match."

Emily smiled. "That was really sweet of you. What did she think?"

Todd laughed. "I went to see her after I did it, and she said I looked better with braids and I wasn't handsome anymore."

Emily laughed, too. "You can't beat kids for being honest." *She might be honest, but she's wrong. You still look good to me,* she thought.

Todd was looking around the kitchen as she was looking at him, examining every inch of his tall, muscular frame. She blushed as he had to repeat his question, since she was in her own little world when he spoke.

"I asked if there was a hotel nearby. I don't want to get in your way," Todd said.

"Todd, don't be silly. There's plenty of room here. Ayanna said you were welcome and you are. She thought the place would be empty because she'd been so busy with her family that she forgot that my camp was last week. We have four bedrooms and two and a half baths, so it doesn't make sense for you to go to a hotel. Just go out to your car and get your things," she said briskly.

"If I'd seen your car I wouldn't have used the key to get in," Todd said ruefully. "I probably just should have waited until I heard you come downstairs or something, instead of just coming in."

"That's because my car is in the barn. And if you hadn't come in you wouldn't have been able to see me in the bathtub, would you?"

Her tone was both casual and naturally seductive, so much so that Todd choked on his lemonade.

"Damn, I'm sorry. I didn't think you heard me upstairs. How did you know I saw you?"

His face got red as she gave him a knowing smile and answered, "Because you just told me. Go get your stuff and I'll take you to your room."

Chapter 3

Alexis couldn't take any more. "Wait a minute, wait a minute! You're telling us that the man saw you naked? *Butt* naked? A strange man saw you with no clothes on, and he's still living? Why didn't you beat the crap out of him?"

Emily shrugged. "He's not a strange man. He's a good friend of my sister. He was a groomsman in her wedding. Don't you remember me telling you about him?"

Sherri and Alexis looked at each other before looking back at her. "No," they answered, once again speaking in unison.

"I must have said something about him," Emily countered. "He's a real nice guy, very handsome, a doctor. Very down-to-earth, too. Are you sure you don't remember?"

"If he was all that, why didn't you get with him when you were in Chicago?" Alexis asked pointedly.

"I don't 'get with' guys, Alexis. That's not my deal. Besides, he was with someone," she answered just as pointedly.

Sherri was shaking her head. "I'm going to forget the naked part for a hot minute, but we're going back to that. If you know the guy and you like him, why did you call the cops on him?"

"I told you, I didn't recognize him! I knew him as having long braids, and they were gone, remember?"

Sherri got up and went to the drawer where Emily kept odds and ends and came back to the table with a notepad and a pen. "I'm going to have a lot of questions when you get through, so I'm taking notes. Alexis, try to hold it in, chick. We need to get the rest of this story before we react."

Alexis moaned dramatically and made a horrible face. Sherri raised an eyebrow and stared her down. Alexis pouted, but the grimace melted away immediately. "That's a good idea, Sherri. I'll try, but I can't promise anything. Okay, what happened next, Em?"

Emily looked totally composed as she watched Todd go out to his car to get his luggage, but nothing could have been further from the truth. After the morning she'd had, her heart was still going like a jackhammer. Her whole world had been turned upside down in the past hour, and she was trying desperately to look as if it was no big deal. But that was going to be really difficult. From the moment she'd met him, Emily had a secret passion for Todd. She'd never shared this information with anyone, especially not him. And now here he was live and in person under her roof. She should have pointed him to the nearest Marriott when he said he'd stay at a hotel, but no, she had to tell him to stay with her. Clearly, she wasn't in her right mind; she was just still rattled from the events of the day.

The moment she'd realized there was someone in the house, she'd gone into panic mode. She'd been singing loudly while she was standing in the bathtub, but she'd caught a glimpse of something out of the corner of her eye that scared the hell out of her. It was a man, a big bald man. She tried to remember if the rifle her father had kept was upstairs where she was or downstairs in the closet. *Downstairs, it's always downstairs,* she muttered. Without bothering to dry off, she got out of the deep tub and tiptoed to her bedroom, leaving the water running so she wouldn't alert the intruder that she'd left the bathroom. Throwing on an old pair of shorts as she reached for her cell phone, she hastily called an old friend of her dad's who happened to be a state trooper in the area. Thankfully he'd been on duty and told her he'd be right there. By the time she'd tossed on a T-shirt, she could see him pull into the driveway behind the strange vehicle that was parked there.

After she tiptoed down the stairs and listened to the man and his partner interrogate the stranger, she realized it was Todd, the man she'd met in Chicago when her sister Ayanna had gotten married. He was tall, intelligent and very funny, as well as fine as hell. When she finally came out on the porch to face him, it took her a few seconds to recognize him because he'd cut off his long braids. He looked like Shemar Moore now, or at least as close to Shemar Moore as she was gonna get. His long lean body was still as sexy as she recalled, and his voice was still as captivating. And he was right here with her on Hilton Head. For once, Emily wished that she had less intellect and more sex appeal, but there was nothing she could do about it now. When Todd returned to the back porch, she held the kitchen door open for him as he carried in a large bag and small duffel.

"I hate to keep repeating myself, but I can easily stay at a hotel," Todd reminded her.

"And I hate to keep telling you that you're perfectly welcome to stay here. Unless you find my company repulsive or something," she replied.

"Ayanna obviously just forgot when I would be here. Even if she'd remembered that I was going to be here, you'd still be welcome. This place is way too big for one person. Come on upstairs and pick out a room so we can get your things put away," she said nonchalantly, as though having a super-fine man drop in on her was an everyday occurrence. Which it wasn't, not by a long shot.

She didn't wait for him to answer; she just started walking to the back stairs that were next to the kitchen. Sucking in air so she wouldn't appear out of breath, which she was due to the faint masculine scent that drifted from Todd, she walked down the hall to the bedroom next to hers.

"You can have your pick of rooms. Daddy wanted this place to hold all of us, plus guests."

The room held a king-size bed, a dresser and armoire, a wide padded window seat and a big comfortable-looking chair. Her mother had decorated it in soothing shades of green, and it looked as posh as a fancy hotel but much homier due to the oak floors and walls. Todd looked around with a satisfied smile. "This is great, Emily. I can't believe your father built this place himself."

"Well, I helped a little. I thought about going into architecture at one time, but science was my real calling." She felt her cheeks grow hot as the shyness that usually overtook her when she was talking to a good-looking man arose. "Okay, I'll let you get settled. I have to get the shampoo out of my hair," she said as she felt the ends, which were getting crispy from the dried suds.

Todd grinned as he saw her fingering her long ringlets. "This time I promise not to spy."

A hot flush raced over her, but this time it didn't reach her face. Rather, it lingered in the most intimate part of her body, and for some reason the feeling wasn't terribly uncomfortable. It was kind of exciting, which made her back out of the room with a quickness. "It wouldn't do you any good, buddy, because I'm locking the door."

Todd's laughter followed her down the hall as she hurried to finish her shower properly.

The day ended much better than it had begun, especially the part with the police raid. After Todd got his things put away, he took a shower in the bathroom that was located safely down the hall from the one Emily was using. He tried valiantly not to think about what she was doing in the other bathroom, but it was impossible. Now that he knew what she looked like under the loose, often baggy clothes that she usually wore, his whole perspective of her had changed. He'd always thought of her as ubersmart, funny and cute as hell, but now he knew the real deal. Emily was a true banger with brains, and it was a dangerous combination. To punish himself for the lustful turn his thoughts were taking, he turned the water to full-on cold, but it didn't help a bit. The erection he'd gotten from thinking about Emily doubled in size in pure defiance.

"Thanks a lot, friend," he mumbled as he turned the water off. "That's just what I need. I've already spied on the woman, and now I'm entertaining thoughts of lust. You need to calm down before you make me do something I'll regret later." Although he couldn't imagine regretting anything he did with Emily. She was so different from the airheaded sexpots he usually wound up with. Anything that transpired between him and Emily would be pure pleasure. He had just finished toweling himself dry when his cell phone rang. He groaned when he saw the number on his caller ID, because it belonged to a woman he had no desire to speak with ever again. He ignored the phone and finished his grooming so he could see what Emily was doing. Whatever it was, it was bound to be as interesting as she was.

Emily took a last look in the mirror before going down to the kitchen. She'd gotten all the shampoo out and put on the leave-in conditioner her sister had forced on her the last time they were together. Makeup and other girly things weren't high on Emily's list of priorities, but she finally agreed with Ayanna on conditioner and a few other basics like clear lip gloss. Her wardrobe was still more functional than feminine, though. She had a vast array of T-shirts and knit tops that she wore with denim for leisure and khakis for work, but that was about it. Even now she was wearing shorts and a tank top with a pair of flip-flops. She looked clean and plain. If she had on some cute earrings or something it might help upgrade her image, but she didn't bring any with her.

"What you see is what you get," she said with a slight frown. She tossed her long, heavy hair over her shoulder and went down to the kitchen to see if there was anything she could make for dinner. The refrigerator door was wide open and she was inspecting the contents when Todd's voice startled her. Two tomatoes hit the floor as he asked if there was anything he could to do to help.

"You can quit sneaking up on me! I'm going to put a bell on you," she said with a frown. "Learn to make some noise when you come into a room."

"I didn't mean to scare you, again," he said with the dazzling smile that made her weak in the knees. "How about I take you out to dinner to make up for it?"

"Well, I was going to make something, but if you want to eat out, we can."

"Wait a minute, you're offering home cooked food? Maybe I should think this over. How good of a cook are you?" He leaned against the counter and continued to show her his dazzling white perfect teeth in his devilish smile.

It was her turn to smile as she answered him. "I cook by the decimal system," she replied.

"I'm not familiar with that," he admitted.

"I can make ten of most things. Ten kinds of cake, ten kinds of sandwiches, ten kinds of salad, you get my drift. I cook basics, like chicken. But I know ten ways to fix it."

"That's, um, different."

Emily shrugged. "Everybody should know how to feed themselves. Ten seemed to be a good number to master. Anything less is boring and anything more is superfluous. So I can fix eggs ten ways. Same with potatoes, tomatoes and just about anything else."

Todd laughed. "Practical and creative, a woman after my own heart. And as much as I'd like to sample some of your decimal kitchen stylings, I'd be less than a gentleman if I didn't take you out. You do like seafood, don't you?"

Emily made a little face. "I love it, but I'm not really dressed to go out. And I can't go change, because I didn't bring anything fancy with me. I don't actually own anything fancy, except the dress I wore in Ayanna's wedding," she said with a hint of defiance.

"So? You look fine to me, and I wasn't thinking about anything fancy. I kinda pictured a dive bar with good food and ice-cold beer. Is there anything like that around here?"

Emily grinned. "If that's what you want, I have just the place for you. Let's go."

"This is just what I had in mind," Todd said approvingly. "Good music, cold beer and great food. And the atmosphere is perfect."

They were seated next to the windows that ran the length of the long, narrow dining room of Fishy's Roadhouse. The walls and floors were of the same weathered wood. The tables were a mixture of old wood and fifties Formica, with worn vinyl chairs. Old license plates and Burma-Shave ads were on the walls, along with stuffed fish and other oddities. A big jukebox was near the bandstand, and "Use Somebody" by the Kings of Leon was playing. The staff wore bowling shirts and jeans, and the total effect was laid-back and cheerful. The food was exceptional, and they had polished off a pile of crab legs and lobster with corn bread, coleslaw and fries. They had also shared a huge slab of pecan pie with Fishy's homemade ice cream.

Todd was enjoying himself tremendously. Emily was totally unselfconscious while she ate, and she ate like a real person, not like the women he dated. They were the salad brigade, women who avoided carbs and red meat and desserts, all the things that made life worth living. Emily had a beautiful body, and she seemed to treat it very well without starving herself. In his experience, a woman who enjoyed the pleasure of eating enjoyed other pleasures as well. From what he could see, Emily was a very sensual lady in all ways. She had a heart-shaped face with rich brown skin that looked as if it would be soft and smooth to touch. Her thick eyebrows were natural, like her eyelashes. That was one of the things he really liked, the fact that she wasn't plastered with makeup. And her smile was just as sexy as she was, with big dimples that bracketed her full, moist lips.

"I'm glad you like this place. I come here all the time when I'm on Hilton Head," she told him. "It's really good in October when the stone crab claws are in season. You can only get them in Florida, but the owner has a relative there and he gets some a few times during the season. They're wonderful, my favorite food."

"How often are you able to get to Hilton Head?" he asked.

"Not as often as I'd like. When I'm not at the university, I'm still busy with community work, like my summer science camp. Or I'm going somewhere else to work. I was in Haiti after the earthquake. I was in New Orleans after Katrina. I never know where I'm going to be," she said. "Recreation gets pushed to the back of the line when it comes to my schedule."

Todd was impressed but curious. "What do you do when you're working in disaster areas? How does your background in biochemistry lend itself to, um…?"

Emily smiled at the way Todd was struggling to word his question. "Don't worry. I'm not experimenting on people or anything. Not too many people know that I'm a medical doctor as well as being a Ph.D. I volunteer for Doctors Without Borders. I usually spend my vacation traveling for the organization."

"Dang girl, you put me to shame," Todd said with obvious sincerity. "Okay, I don't understand how a woman like you is still single. Are you sure there isn't some big jealous guy who's gonna come looking for you and try to split my skull? You are probably the most accomplished person I've ever met," he said with eyes full of admiration.

Emily gave him a slight side eye. "That's the kind of question a woman would ask, Todd. You sound like you don't know much about your own species. When has career accomplishment ever been a criterion for male attraction?"

Todd looked surprised at her blunt tone. "Well, now that all depends on the man. Some men like prime rib and some like burgers," he began.

Emily held up her hand as she rolled her eyes.

"Really, Todd? You're comparing me to meat? I think we need to go home so you can have some quiet time. You're venturing into some real scary territory," she said with a smile.

Todd returned her grin with one of his own. "You're right. Let's get out of here before I put my other foot in my mouth." He left a generous tip and they departed. Even though he'd been warned, he had to make an additional comment as they walked to the car. "I stand by what I said. You're the whole package, Ms. Emily, which is why I can't understand why you're single."

She groaned and shook her head. "Why is marriage supposed to be this big prize? Why is it like the most important thing in the world for a woman? I could ask you the same thing, you know. You're not married, so what's up with that?"

Todd had to smile as he put his arm around her shoulder. "That's a good question, and I'm going to give you a good answer as soon as I think of one."

"You'd better think hard, because I have a well-honed B.S. detector built into my head," she cautioned him.

"Duly noted. I'll never try to get over on you in any way," he vowed.

"Don't even worry about it, Todd. I wouldn't let you get over on me anyway."

Chapter 4

The rest of the evening was a lot of fun, as well as being a revelation for Todd. When they reached the house, they were still bantering back and forth about a number of things, and Todd discovered that Emily had a wicked sense of humor. She also had great taste in TV, as far as he was concerned.

"We don't bother with cable since we're not here daily, but we have lots of DVDs. Do you like *True Blood*? I've got the box set," Emily told him. "The first two seasons."

"That show is the only reason I got a DVR," Todd said reverently. "Well, not the only one, but one of them."

Emily handed him the DVD with a smile. "You've got good taste in TV. That bit of good taste just about makes up for the meat thing. I'm going to make popcorn."

Todd watched her cute behind and long shapely legs as she went to the kitchen, and he smiled. He was putting the disc into the player when his cell phone rang. The sight of the name on his caller ID made him frown, and he quickly pushed the Ignore button.

"Screening calls? She's not going to like that," Emily teased him.

Todd got up from the couch and took the large tray she was carrying from her hands. "Maybe *you* need to have a bell on. Okay, I get the sneaking up thing. I promise I'll stomp from now on. Thanks for the popcorn. Now can we please just watch *True Blood?*"

"Just ignore my question, that's fine," she said with a laugh. "I love this show," she added, adroitly changing the subject.

"So you're really into supernatural stuff?"

"Absolutely. I like paranormal, sci-fi, horror, espionage and action, anything like that."

"No chick flicks? I thought most women liked them. My sisters love them," Todd said.

Emily made a face. "I think my mom might have some here, but it's not a genre I'm particularly interested in." She picked up the remote and pushed play.

"You're an interesting woman, Emily Porter."

"Yeah, that's what they tell me."

Emily couldn't remember when she'd felt so good. Nor could she recall the sofa being so comfortable. It was a big, cushy wraparound sectional, but tonight its cushions felt sensational and they smelled good, too. Her eyelids felt curiously heavy as she leaned in closer to get a good sniff of the heavenly fragrance. It was fresh and masculine and it certainly wasn't Febreze, but it smelled familiar. It smelled just like, like Todd. Her eyes opened wide and she realized that she'd been curled up next to him with her head on his shoulder, sniffing him like an eager puppy. Heat flooded her face as he looked down at her.

"You're back with me, huh? I thought you were out for the night," he teased.

Emily sat up and tried to disentangle herself from Todd's long arms, but he didn't seem too eager to let her go. She gave a final tug so that she was able to put some space between their bodies.

"How long have I been asleep?" she asked grumpily. She felt her hair and sighed when she realized she had bed head. Running her fingers through it, she gave his T-shirt a look. "I didn't drool on you, did I?"

Todd laughed; a low, sexy sound. "No, you didn't drool. You started getting quiet, and the next thing I know you had nodded out. You missed the second disc in its entirety," he informed her.

"You should have shaken me or punched me or something," she said.

"First of all, that's not how I would treat a lady, ever. Second, I was enjoying it. Your hair smells good and you're nice and warm."

Emily felt heat surge up again at his words. It wasn't just because she was embarrassed; it was because she was aroused. She'd dreamed about him on more than one occasion, and the experience of having him so close to her in real life was wreaking havoc with her senses. The fact that he was looking at her with such a sexy expression on his face wasn't helping, either. If anything, it was making her temperature rise faster than she could handle, and she reacted the way she normally did when confronted with the unfamiliar: she snapped at Todd.

"Yeah. I'm going to lock up and I'm going to bed. Good night," she said irritably. She stood up on feet that were uncharacteristically unsteady and winced as Todd stood up to support her. His strong hands encircled her waist, and she had to bite her lip to keep from saying something she'd regret for life.

"Wait, I'll go with you. I think I locked the

doors, but you can show me how to do it right. This is a beautiful place, but it's so far off the main road. You should get a dog for protection," he said as he walked with her to the front door.

Emily checked the heavy locks to make sure they were both secure. "This is a very low crime area and I can take care of myself," she said grumpily.

Todd didn't seem put off by her tone in the least. "Everybody thinks that until something happens. They think they can handle anything and they get caught off guard, just like you did today," he reminded her.

She stopped walking so abruptly that he bumped into her. She unlocked a tall walnut cabinet in the hallway just outside the kitchen. It was her father's gun safe, and the contents were intimidating, to say the least. There were two rifles and two shotguns, and cloth-lined drawers held his handguns. Emily deftly removed a handgun and closed the door to the safe.

"My dad was a hunter and he taught me how to shoot when I was quite young. I still go to the range every other month just to make sure my skills are what they should be. I normally keep one in the nightstand, but I forgot to take one out when I got here. That's good news for you, because you would have had this little thing pointed at you instead of having a conversation with a couple of nice, reasonable officers," she informed him with an evil smile.

Todd reached over and took the gun from her so quickly she didn't have time to react. "I don't like guns. You need a big dog."

Emily didn't know whether to be outraged at his calm demeanor or turned on by his utter masculinity. She took a stab at outrage and crossed her arms to commence the verbal beat-down that was her usual weapon with macho-acting men.

"I don't know who you think you are, but I'm trained and licensed to carry that weapon, and it belongs to me. How dare you…" Her voice trailed off as he politely put the gun on top of the gun safe.

His hands came down on her shoulders, and he tilted her face up to his. "I'm sure you're just as capable with a handgun as you are with everything else, but I still don't like the idea of you coming here by yourself and relying on an arsenal for safety. I don't want anything to happen to you, Emily."

She was afraid her knees were going to buckle. He was looking at her with utter sincerity and concern, two things she wasn't used to seeing in a man's eyes. Clearly she was out of her element here, but her traitorous body was actually enjoying the way he was making her feel. Her eyelids started to close and she prepared herself to feel his mouth against hers.

"Let's finish locking up so you can get to bed. You look a little sleepy," Todd said.

Emily turned quickly and made sure the kitchen door was locked, as well as the windows she'd opened earlier. She showed Todd how to use the house's alarm system, and once everything was secured, they went upstairs. Her heartbeat had returned to normal and she was calm enough to speak in a casual manner.

"Good night, Todd. I hope you're comfortable. If you hear anything in the morning, it'll just be me. I leave the house at about seven to run."

His face brightened. "Can I join you? I usually use a treadmill for convenience, but I love to run outside."

"If you want to, but I get up at six-thirty," she cautioned him.

"Not a problem. Sleep well."

Her hand was on her doorknob as she looked up at him. "You, too. Sleep well, I mean."

Without warning he leaned down and took her mouth with his for a lingering kiss that rocked her to her very soul.

"Now I will," he said.

Todd might have slept soundly, but Emily was having a very difficult time in her room. Ever since Todd had kissed her she'd been dizzy. His lips were hot and smooth and strong, and she'd never felt anything like them in her life. She wasn't a virgin and she'd had some pleasurable sexual experiences in the past, but they paled in comparison to the thrill of Todd's kiss. It was unexpected, sweet and hot as fire, and she could still feel it as she tossed and turned in bed.

She had stripped off her clothes as soon as she got into her room, changing into an old plaid cotton robe that she'd had since college. It was big and baggy and utterly hideous, but she needed to be completely covered because she needed a shower right now, preferably a cold one that would shock her back into her right mind. After bundling her hair up into a knot, she waited until she was sure Todd was in his room for the night and she slipped out into the hallway and scooted to the bathroom. Turning the water on full blast, she lathered her body from head to toe, trying to put out the fire Todd had lit.

Why did he kiss me, she wondered. And why didn't he do it again? He didn't have to stop; they could have kept on kissing until morning as far as she was concerned. Better yet, they could have just kissed their way into her bed. She was honest enough to admit that she'd desired him since the day they'd met, way back when Ayanna got married. They were introduced at the wedding rehearsal, and she could still recall every detail of their meeting. Everything was engraved in her memory, from what he had on, how he smelled, what his skin felt like as they shook hands to his beautiful smile. She'd had an instant attraction to him, but she was far too self-conscious and shy to make her interest known.

Her feelings about Todd would have remained a secret forever if he hadn't turned up on her doorstep. But he had, and in a few hours he'd gone from being an abstract desire to something else. What that something was, she wasn't sure. It wasn't possible to put a name on it. He'd seen her naked, she'd called the police on him; they'd had a nice dinner and watched a DVD until she fell asleep in his arms. She'd waved a gun in his face, and he kissed her good-night. As a first day together it was interesting, to say the least. What would tomorrow bring?

She licked her lips and experienced the same vestigial thrill she'd been feeling since Todd had kissed her. Whatever came next, she vowed she'd be ready for it. Opportunities like this came only once in a lifetime and she wasn't going to waste it.

Chapter 5

The next morning Todd hoped he didn't look as tired as he felt. The bed was comfortable and he had no trouble going to sleep, but the highly erotic dreams he had about Emily kept waking him up in the various stages of desire and plain old horniness. It was his fault, he freely admitted. He shouldn't have kissed her, because finding out how good she could do it drove him crazy when he was supposed to be getting a good night's slumber. Considering the fact that he'd committed to getting up at an ungodly hour to run with her, he should have gotten a lot more sleep. After splashing a lot of cold water on his face in an attempt to look more alert than he was feeling, he pulled on a baggy pair of shorts and a ratty tank top that had seen better days and went down the back stairs to the kitchen. After taking one look at Emily, he was alert all over.

"Good morning," she said. "You want some grape juice and toast? I can't run on an empty stomach."

"Sure, but I'll get it. You look cute, by the way."

She turned red, which made her look even cuter. Her long thick hair was pulled up in a braided ponytail so that her graceful neck was exposed, and she had on red runner's shorts that showed off her strong, shapely legs. A snug-fitting white racer-back bra top completed her ensemble, and she looked delicious.

"Thanks," she mumbled. "It looks like it's gonna rain, so we should probably hit it. I'm going to go warm up," she added as she headed for the door.

Todd went to the window to watch her. It was overcast, as she said, but he still ate two pieces of multigrain toast and downed a glass of juice. Like Emily, he had to have something in his stomach before exercising. Besides that, he was enjoying the view. Emily was incredibly limber as she stretched her long legs. All the twists and turns she was doing were accelerating his heart rate better than a warm-up. She presented entirely too much temptation for this hour of the morning. Something crossed his mind, and he went out to take it up with Emily.

"Do you always run by yourself?" he asked abruptly.

Emily looked at him strangely. "When I'm here, yes, I do. When I'm at home I run on campus, and there're usually other people out there on the track. Why?"

"You look a little too good to be out here by yourself. That's another reason to get a dog. Protection," he said gruffly.

"Are you kidding? You need to get a hobby or something, Todd. That way you won't be wasting time worrying about nonsense. I can take care of myself. Get warmed up or I'll leave you," she warned.

He gave her a look which said the conversation wasn't over, but he started his warm-up. As he started stretching his torso, Emily gasped.

"Todd, what happened to you? Where did you get those scars from?"

He gave her a faint semblance of a smile and pulled the tank top off so she could see the scars that went from his shoulder to his breastbone. There were three of them, and the recent removal of the sutures was quite evident.

"These are battle wounds. I was at work on a gang member in the E.R. when someone from the other gang jumped off his gurney and snatched a scalpel. His target was my patient, but when I blocked him he decided to come at me. Nice, huh?"

He was both alarmed and touched when her eyes filled with tears and she covered her mouth with a shaking hand. "Why didn't anyone tell me?"

"Don't be upset," he said. "It wasn't that big a deal. Ayanna probably didn't mention it to you because the twins were under the weather and she had her hands full. Besides, I was only in the hospital for a couple of days and it was all over," he said soothingly.

Emily didn't seem to be listening to his words. She was tracing the scars with a gentle hand. Suddenly her expression turned stern and she pointed a finger at him. "You're giving me grief about being safe, and you got attacked while you were at work. Kind of hypocritical of you, wouldn't you agree?"

Todd pulled the tank top on again. "That's my point exactly! There's no telling what can happen to you at any time, anyplace, so you need to be careful. If you had a dog for protection, you'd be safer."

"Like you were at your place of work?"

"A gang war in Chicago isn't exactly the norm for my place of work," he began.

"Liar! You work in the busiest E.R. in the city of Chicago, and the crime rate there is pretty darned high, so you have an outstanding chance of being in a dangerous situation any day of the week," she said hotly. "Looks like you're the one who needs to be more careful, not me."

Todd tried not to smile, but it was difficult. She looked so adorable as she argued him down, her feminine appeal was irresistible. Plus, it was obvious that she cared about what happened to him, which was touching even as she told him off. The only way to shut her up was another kiss, which he willingly applied. He reached for her, pulled her to his chest and put his lips over hers. She stiffened for a second before relaxing against him and letting the magic happen. Her tongue tasted vaguely of grape juice, but more like pure sugar. He ran his hands up and down her exposed back until she sighed and leaned into him as her hands returned his caress. The kiss would have gone on much longer, but the overcast sky let loose with a torrent of rain. When the big warm drops of water got to be too much to ignore, they had to abandon passion and run back to the house.

They were both laughing when a brilliant flash of lightning brightened the sky to herald a crash of thunder.

"So much for my morning run," Emily said as she wiped drops of moisture from her face with a kitchen towel.

"Yeah, it's a wrap for now," Todd agreed as he looked at her lithe figure with ill-disguised desire.

Her top was thoroughly wet and her nipples were pointing through the supple knit fabric. "So now what do we do?"

Emily licked her lips and touched her damp ponytail. "I think we should get out of these clothes," she murmured.

Todd grinned and moved closer to her while he ripped off his tank top for the second time that morning. "I agree."

Her face flushed and her nipples were even more prominent as he continued to walk toward her.

Emily was relieved when her cell phone rang, because if he'd taken one more step she was pretty sure she'd have lost all control. It was her sister Ayanna, calling to let her know that Todd was going to be using the house.

"Thanks for the heads-up, Ayanna, but you're a day late with that information. Todd got here yesterday."

"Here where? Where are you, Emily?" Ayanna sounded totally confused, which amused Emily to no end.

"I'm here in Hilton Head with Todd. My science camp was last week and I came here to recuperate. Those kids wore me out," Emily told her.

"Ohhh, sweetie! You don't mind him being there, do you? I had no idea you were there," Ayanna said apologetically.

"Oh, I'm fine with it, although you should be asking him if it's all right if I'm here, since I was the one who called the police on him," Emily said cheerily.

"You did *what?*" Ayanna screeched so loudly that Emily had to hold the phone away from her ear.

"It's a long story and I'll be happy to tell you all about it later. It's all good, though. Do you want to talk to him, to make sure I'm not mistreating him?" Emily said with a laugh.

"Not right now. I'm trying to get the girls dressed, and that can take a while. They like to pick out their own clothes now, and it's quite a production," Ayanna told her.

Emily smiled at the thought of her twin nieces. They were two years old and just amazing. "How are my nieces and nephews?"

"Everyone is fine. The boys are doing great in school and the twins are growing like weeds. You'll see for yourself when you come up here. I'll talk to you later, sweetie."

Emily was smiling as she ended the call. She and her older sister had developed a closeness that had seemed impossible at one time. Now they were friends as well as relatives, something she found very satisfying.

When she ended the call, she found Todd looking at her intently. "What?"

"I was just thinking you might want to get into some dry clothes," he said. "And I was thinking I should make you breakfast."

Emily's clothes were unpleasantly damp from the rain and she was a little self-conscious about her scanty attire, since they weren't running. And the toast and juice seemed like hours ago. She was ravenous, for some reason. "That sounds like a plan. Can you cook?"

"You can give me your opinion after you eat," Todd said with a smile. "Let's get out of these wet clothes and I'll do my best to amaze you."

It didn't take long for Emily to take a quick hot shower and change into dry clothing, but she dragged it out as long as she could. She was still processing the fact that Todd had kissed her *again,* and the second time was way more sensual than the first. How was she supposed to get her head around the idea that she was under the same roof as her fantasy man? And that he'd put his arms around her and kissed her not once, but twice? She sat down heavily on the chair next to the window and watched the rain come down. She wasn't used to lighthearted flirting and frivolity with handsome men. Relationships with serious-minded scientists were basically what she knew of romance and sex. She'd only been involved with men she'd known for a while, men who respected her as a colleague. This business with Todd wasn't exactly in her comfort zone.

The smell of bacon floated up the stairs and reminded her that she was hungry. She had a keen appetite for food and for Todd, too, if she was going to be honest with herself. She finally stood up and walked over to the dresser to look in the mirror. A blue plaid shirt, jeans and some ancient Birkenstock sandals with her unruly hair held back by a headband; that was as good as she was going to get. She didn't see her perfect skin, the deep Cupid's bow that made her mouth irresistible and her beautiful eyes. All she saw was the same geeky science nerd she'd seen most of her life. The rich scent of coffee joined the other cooking aromas and her stomach took control. With a small sigh she left the room and headed for the back stairs. At least one of her appetites would be taken care of—or so she hoped. Entering the kitchen, she took a deep sniff and said, "I hope this tastes as good as it smells, or you could be in deep trouble."

Todd gave her another blisteringly sexy smile. "Come see for yourself. Have a seat," he invited.

She did so at once, trying to act casual when he held her chair and slid it in as if this was something they did all the time. He had set the table and poured her coffee as well as juice, this time orange. There was a fluffy omelet on her plate, along with a serving of buttery grits. A small plate held heavenly smelling cinnamon toast, and there was a bowl of cantaloupe chunks at each place.

"Wow, this looks really good, Todd. I'm impressed."

He took his seat across from her and held out his hand to take hers. "I hope it's to your liking. We'd better say grace so you don't get ptomaine poisoning or something."

Emily gave him a mischievous grin. "That's probably wise. Everything that looks good to you isn't necessarily good for you."

"Damn, Emmie, that was harsh."

She had to take back her words after she cut into the tender omelet with her fork. It was perfect, filled with diced potatoes, red peppers, onions, cheese and tomatoes. It was probably the best omelet she'd ever eaten. A groan of pleasure escaped her mouth before she realized it.

"This is so good," she sighed. The cinnamon toast was a real treat, crisp and golden brown on the edges and moist inside with just the right amount of cinnamon sugar on the top. "Where did you learn to cook like this?"

"A starving student can learn to do anything. I don't do much besides breakfast, but I do breakfast well."

"Yes, you do. Best I've had in a long time," Emily said appreciatively.

Todd gave her a smoldering look and asked, "So how do you plan to repay me?"

Unfortunately, his words came right after she took a big swallow of orange juice and she choked on it, sending a fine spray everywhere. He laughed, to her chagrin, and she glared at him from her end of the table. It looked as if the pleasant part of the morning was over.

Chapter 6

It continued to rain all day, but it felt as if the sun was out at the beach house. Todd had apologized for his laughter and explained what his comment meant.

"I wasn't trying to say anything scandalous, I promise. I was going to ask if you were going to wash dishes since I'd cooked, that's all."

Emily had felt rather foolish when she heard his simple explanation, but he could see that and wasn't about to let her feel bad.

"I tell you what, I'll wash and you dry, how's that?" he asked.

"No, I'll clean up the kitchen. It's only fair since

you made me this nice meal," she said. She bit into a juicy piece of cantaloupe and sighed in repletion. "This is so good. It's perfectly ripe and sweet. I think cantaloupe is a much underrated fruit."

Surprisingly, Todd agreed with her. "Yeah, watermelon gets all the shine, but cantaloupe is really bomb. It's got the best taste and the smoothest texture, but people don't seem to realize that. When it's ripe and ready, it's the best fruit out there in my opinion."

He was just talking about fruit, but for some reason Emily started feeling hot, bothered and moist in some truly inappropriate places. She ate the rest of the fruit in a hurry and got up gracelessly to start clearing the table, but Todd stopped her.

"Slow down, baby. It's not like we're going anywhere," he said as he looked out the window at the rain continuing to pour. A loud clap of thunder underscored his words. "We can take our time with this. The dishes aren't going anywhere."

Emily gave an exaggerated sigh and put her hand to her heart. "I have a confession to make, Todd. I'm a total neat freak. I can't stand to have anything out of place. I know it borders on OCD, but I've been this way since I was a kid," she said apologetically.

"There's nothing wrong with being organized.

I could use some of that myself," Todd admitted. "Okay, let's get this knocked out so we can relax."

In a very short time the kitchen was sparkling clean. "So what do we do now? What do you like to do when you're not working?" Todd asked.

Emily leaned against the counter and thought about the question. "When I'm here I like to walk on the beach and swim and read on the porch. I ride my bike or watch DVDs, nothing too thrilling."

"Sounds good to me. Since we can't walk or swim or go outside, we can watch movies," Todd suggested.

Emily gave him a wry smile. "This isn't what you had in mind when you decided to take a vacation, is it? You're going to be bored out of your mind."

He looked surprised and said, "Are you crazy? This is way better than anything I could have planned. I pick the movie this time."

It was Emily's turn to look surprised as he took her hand and led her to the big family room. She sat on the sofa while he perused the DVDs and selected one. It gave her an opportunity to take a good long look at him. He really was fine, even in a pair of old jeans and an equally ancient T-shirt. Probably the best looking man she'd ever known as well as being one of the nicest and damnably sexy to boot. *He should come with a warning label,* she thought. *Warning: contents of this hot body should be considered dangerous.*

She was laughing softly when he placed the DVD into the player and came to join her on the couch. "What's so funny?"

"Nothing," she said. "What are we watching?"

"The Godfather," he said in his best Marlon Brando imitation, which wasn't too good. This time she laughed out loud.

"It's a good thing you're a doctor, because you wouldn't make it as an actor," she said as she wiped her eyes.

Todd moved so that his thigh was pressed against hers. He put his arm around her neck and brought her face closer to his. "That was cruel. Quiet down, woman, and watch the movie."

"Yes, Godfather," she said and collapsed in giggles as he growled into her hair.

They did more talking than watching the movie. Emily got up at one point to get a big bowl of pistachios and a bottle of white grape juice.

"It was as close as I could get to a bottle of wine," she said. "Something about this movie always makes me want to drink wine, but it's way too early for alcohol."

Todd agreed with a smile. "Good point. We wouldn't want to get tipsy and do something crazy," he said.

Emily took a healthy swallow from her glass.

"What constitutes as crazy? Robbing a convenience store, stealing a car or making mad, passionate love all afternoon?" she asked. Her face flushed as she realized what she'd just said.

Todd didn't seem to think there was anything wrong with her question. On the contrary, he answered it easily. "Committing a felony or two would be crazy, but making love would be completely sane. Especially if I was making love to you," he said in the sexy voice that was beginning to drive her crazy.

She was too flustered to respond and picked a few nuts out of the bowl. Todd leaned into her side to get her attention. "I said, making love to you…"

"I heard you," Emily said irritably. "Pay attention to the movie or put in another one."

"Ms. Emily, I believe I've embarrassed you, which wasn't my intention. Suppose I told you I was trying to be seductive?"

"I'd say you were crazy. I'm not even sure men can be seductive. Isn't that what women do?" she mumbled.

"I don't think it's gender specific. If a man wants to make love to a pretty, intriguing woman whom he finds irresistible, he has to make her as interested in him as he is in her. Men have been seducing women forever, Emmie."

"And what does that have to do with me? I'm

not the kind of woman who gets seduced," she said with a frown.

"Don't be too sure of that. From my perspective, you're the perfect candidate. You're brilliant, funny and beautiful, and you're sexy as hell," he told her.

"You're pretty funny yourself. I would have gone for brilliant and funny, but sexy and beautiful? That's laying it on a little thick, don't you think?" She put the pistachio shells into a smaller bowl and wiped her hands on her jeans to get rid of the salt from the nuts. "Let's change the subject, shall we? It looks like it's stopped raining, so why don't we go for a quick ride? I was going to get a chicken for dinner."

Without waiting for his answer, she got up and collected the bowls and glasses from the coffee table. She was leaving the room when she heard Todd call after her. "You can run but you can't hide. We're going to finish this conversation sooner or later."

Later, she thought. *So much later it's going to be never.*

Several hours later, the awkwardness had faded away and Emily and Todd were sitting side by side on the cushioned glider on the screened-in porch. They relaxed as they digested Emily's wonderful meal and sipped wine. Todd was still raving about the roast chicken.

"I'm definitely adding cooking to your growing list of attributes. That chicken was perfect."

"It was just plain roast chicken with green beans and mashed cauliflower. I'm glad you liked it, but it was no big deal," she said modestly.

"Stop being so humble," Todd scolded. "I once read that the mark of a great cook is how they cook the basics, like a chicken. Yours was moist and tender and perfectly seasoned. And I've never had pureed cauliflower before, but it was gooder than grits, baby. The flavor is really different, way better than mashed potatoes. You got some mad skillz in the kitchen, Emmie."

"Thanks. Do you want some more wine?"

"Absolutely. This is really good, by the way. What is it again?"

"Moscato. I fell in love with it last summer, and I don't usually like sweet wine. But this is totally delicious for some reason. It's cheap and it goes well with most everything, even though it's really a dessert wine," she murmured.

The rain had come back, making the evening air cool and refreshing. Emily had lit some nag champa incense and the heavy scent, mixed with the smell of the rain, was as intoxicating as the wine. Todd was so close to her that she was getting aroused from the warmth of his body. She loved the smell of his skin. It was like an aphrodisiac to her, so much so that it gave her goose bumps. She shivered and Todd put his arm around her.

"Are you getting cold? Maybe we should go inside," he said. "I wouldn't want you to catch a cold."

She gave a small snort of laughter. "Nobody wants that," she assured him. "It's not a pretty sight, I promise you. I look like fresh hell when I'm under the weather."

Todd buried his nose in her soft, fragrant hair. "Impossible. As fine as you are, you could never look bad."

Emily rolled her eyes and quickly rose from the glider. She stubbed out the incense and blew out the candles she'd lit earlier. The pleasant mood was most definitely broken.

Todd got up and joined her, retrieving the wine bottle and their glasses before following her into the house. "Emily, why do you react like that every time I pay you a compliment?"

"Because it's been my experience that compliments are just another form of B.S. I told you I have a built-in radar for crap, and you're setting it off."

They were back in the family room and she was fiddling with the gas fireplace. Todd shook his head at the sight of her deliberate effort to turn away from him. He put the glasses and bottle down and went to where she was standing. Putting his hands on her shoulders, he turned her around and held her close to his body.

"I don't know if that's a reflection on you or on me, but I can assure you I'm not trying to shine you on or anything close to it. I'm trying to let you know how attracted I am to you. I've always found you to be captivating, but the timing was always off."

"Horseshit," she murmured. He was just a little too close to her for comfort, and she couldn't come up with anything clever to say.

Todd ignored her unladylike comment and kept talking.

"When I first met you at Ayanna's wedding I thought you were adorable, but I was involved with someone at the time," he said as he began to play with her hair.

Emily closed her eyes and bit her lower lip to prevent a low purr of contentment from escaping. "I've been in Chicago several times since the wedding," she said in a near-whisper.

Todd moved closer to her, kissing her temple and her cheek. "I know exactly how many times you've been to Chicago. I put every single visit on my calendar because I made a point of coming over so I could see you."

"So why didn't you say something to me about

this big attraction?" Her voice was partially muffled by his chest and husky from desire.

"Bad timing." He kissed her cheeks again, lingering on her tempting dimples and the bridge of her nose before capturing her mouth. His tongue stroked her lower lip as her mouth opened to him. He had no intention of ending this kiss, and neither did she. His hands slid down her taut torso and cupped her high, firm butt, palming her so that their bodies met and locked together.

"Bad timing?" she murmured as he licked her neck. "How's our time right now?"

"Just perfect," Todd answered between kisses.

"So why are we still downstairs?"

Todd's response was to pick her up and head for the stairs with her legs around his waist. In minutes they were in her bedroom, tearing at each other's clothes.

Chapter 7

Todd was trying to be patient, but he couldn't wait for her fingers to undo all of his buttons. He ripped off his shirt and tossed it to the floor while he undid his belt and unzipped his jeans. Emily knelt on the bed and watched him with passion-filled eyes while she took off her shirt. Her rounded breasts were already reacting to the sight of him, as her nipples were hardened and erect beneath the knit cups of her white bra. She was about to undo the front hook when Todd stopped her. He undid the closure with surprising ease and freed her high, perfect globes to his hands and mouth. He bent down and took a nipple into his mouth, making a sound of pleasure as he tasted her. He was busy unfastening her jeans while he traced circles around the tip of her hot breast, sucking on it until she cried his name. He freed her from her jeans and ran his hands down her hips before lowering her to the mattress.

She looked hotter than anything he could have imagined. Her thick hair was tousled wildly, and the only thing she was wearing were bikini panties in white cotton. They looked adorable on her, besides being way sexier than any of the lacy thongs he'd seen in the past. And he'd seen plenty, but none that aroused him as much as he was right now. Her hips arched as he pulled the panties down, leaving her naked and yielding to his touch. He had to taste her; all of her, right then and there.

Todd guided her long legs over his shoulders and cupped her round, firm butt as he moved into a position that allowed him to take his first taste of the wet sweetness that awaited him. As soon as his tongue made contact with her, a sound of passion came from her throat as she moved her hips in a perfect rhythm with his mouth. He could feel the pulsing warmth of her womanhood getting hotter and wetter, and he knew the moment she came. It took him only seconds to change positions so that he could enter her. She was hot, tight and throbbing, and the way it felt to his manhood made him groan with pleasure. He tried to hold off his climax until she was near hers, and in minutes they were both spent and satisfied.

When he could move again, he rolled over so that they were still joined but lying on their sides, facing each other. He kissed her, slowly and with great tenderness. "I think I rushed you," he murmured.

Emily smiled at him, her eyes soft and sexy. "What do you mean?"

"I mean I should have taken my time and gotten to know each and every delectable part of you," he confessed. "You deserve more."

"Really?" Emily's hand stroked his chest, her fingertips just barely grazing his smooth, sweaty skin. Without any more effort than that, she was sending small bolts of sensation through his body. "Exactly what is it that I deserve?" she asked.

By way of an answer, he leaned over and kissed her deeply, using his tongue and lips to communicate with her in a way that words could not. He was taking his time, slowly exploring her body as he promised, using his big hands to rub her breasts as he kissed his way down her neck and shoulder until his hot lips reached her nipples. They were hard and enlarged as proof of her desire. His tongue circled one over and over until his mouth covered it completely, and he created a deep suction that drew a sigh of pure pleasure from Emily.

This time, Todd would not hurry. He took an

excruciatingly long time to touch and taste every single part of Emily's body. She was almost sobbing his name before her entered her again, but the sweet torture was worth it to both of them. It was as though he was depositing his soul into her as they climaxed together.

Emily couldn't recall being so content with a man before. Todd's brand of lovemaking had taken her to a whole new level of satisfaction. She stretched like a cat and sighed, which caused Todd to ask if she was okay.

"Gee, let's see," she said with a drowsy laugh. "I'm in a bathtub full of bubbles, surrounded by scented candles, serenaded by soft music and being seduced by a tall, dark and handsome man who seems to have memorized the Kama Sutra, and you want to know if I'm okay. Are you fishing for a compliment?"

Todd was lying back in the huge tub with Emily resting between his legs, her back snugly against his chest. He stroked her round, firm breasts and gave them a gentle squeeze as he answered. "Naw, I'm just making sure that you're happy," he drawled. "And I haven't memorized the Kama Sutra. I read the first chapter when I was like, twelve. It was kinda boring, but the pictures were pretty hot."

Emily laughed as she ran her hands up and

down his hard, muscular thighs. "That was cute. You made it up, but it was pretty funny."

Todd's long fingers deepened the massage on one of her breasts, with his thumb circling her hard nipple, while his other hand explored the hot, sweet place between her legs. "I never lie, baby. I got the book from my brother's hiding place under his mattress. And I have an excellent memory for detail, like sexually explicit drawings."

Her back arched as she moved her hips to the motion of his hand. Heat surged up her body and radiated through every bit of her. It was a slow burn that suddenly flared up as he took her back to the place of pleasure and surrender. She breathed his name, and he couldn't resist teasing her gently.

"Do you still think I made it up?"

"No!" she gasped. "I believe you, I believe you, I believe you," she moaned until she couldn't utter another sound.

After some more passion, they finally managed to get out of the tub. They were both starving, and Emily was fairly certain that if she did some of the things she wanted to do to Todd, she'd drown in the scented water. They finally made their way to the kitchen, although they weren't fully dressed. Emily had on the silk kimono her mother had given her a couple of years before. Todd was shirtless in a pair of cotton drawstring sleep pants that hung low on his hips. He looked so good that Emily considered forcing him onto the bed to have her way with him some more, but his stomach growled loudly and she decided to have mercy on him.

She opened the refrigerator to see what looked appetizing. Todd was looking too, but he was mostly looking at Emily and playing with her hair.

"How about I make you a sandwich?" she asked. "I can make really good ones."

"Ten different kinds, if I recall," he replied. "Yeah, that's good. I happen to love a good sandwich."

She was taking out what she thought she'd need; deli-sliced roast beef, a red ripe tomato, an avocado, some arugula and green goddess salad dressing. She almost dropped everything when Todd told her how much he liked her hair.

"It's so soft and pretty. I love it," he told her.

Emily's cheeks got hot, and she felt totally flustered. She'd almost forgotten that her hair was loose and damp from their bath and subsequent shower. *Pretty my ass,* she thought. *I probably look like a damned Muppet.*

Despite her misgivings, Todd actually seemed sincere in his compliments. He was still stroking what she was sure was a tangled nappy mess, but he was apparently fascinated with her tresses. "You don't put any chemicals in it, do you? It's all natural," he marveled.

"No, I've never had a relaxer. I don't press it and I've never had it cut. I just braid it and go. I don't have time to mess with it," she said grumpily. She wasn't used to much attention, especially from a gorgeous man like Todd, and it was making her uncomfortable. Getting out the cutting board, she slapped a loaf of pumpernickel bread on its wooden surface and reached for a bread knife to slice it. Todd stopped talking about her dratted hair long enough to wash his hands at the sink. Unfortunately for her, he started talking again while he was drying his hands.

"You don't need to do anything to it. It's perfect just the way it is. Most women would mess it up with stanky chemicals, but you have the good sense to leave it like God gave it to you. You're one of the most beautiful women I've ever seen in my life, and you're a totally natural beauty. Just gorgeous," he added.

By now Emily would normally have said something mean and smart-asslike to him to deflect her embarrassment, but for once she held her tongue. Her cheeks felt as if they were on fire and she couldn't quite look him in the eye, but she was finally enjoying his flattery. It was like getting a cold drink of water after a long hot run; it was something she desired and deserved, and she was going to savor every drop. She finally looked at him with a shy smile on her face.

"Thank you, Todd. That was very sweet of you to say."

Todd came up behind her and wrapped his arms around her. "That was nice of you, babe, but never thank me for telling the truth. You can feed me," he added pointedly. "Especially if you plan on taking advantage of me again." He let go of her just enough to move her hair out of the way so he could kiss her neck, which he did with great skill and desire.

"You'd better stop that if you plan to eat, because I can assure you I have plans for you," she said in a sultry voice.

He turned her around so they were facing each other, and he pressed the lower part of his body into hers. "On second thought, I can wait a little while longer for food, but I still need to eat. Have you ever made love in a kitchen?"

Chapter 8

Emily finally stopped her narrative long enough
to finish her glass of wine. Her two BFFs were
staring at her raptly with their mouths slightly
open. Sherri was the first to recover.

"Wait a minute, girl. You can't just stop talking
like that. It's cruel and unusual punishment! What
else happened?"

Alexis agreed emphatically. "Okay, so far you
haven't said anything that explains why you're in
such a foul mood. Shoot, it sounds to me like you
were having a great time on Hilton Head with Mr.
Man. So who peed in your Kool-Aid, sister? Did
he pick his teeth at the table, pass gas in his sleep,
call you by somebody else's name or what?"

Emily was rolling the stem of her wineglass back and forth with her fingertips. "Nope, nothing like that," she said quietly.

Sherri made a face from sheer frustration. "I love you, Em, but you need to talk faster. I'm with Alexis on this one. So far everything you told us sounds like it's straight out of a Janice Sims novel. Or a Brenda Jackson book, you fast little heifer." She left the table to get something out of her large purse and came back with a sneaky smile on her face. "I have some extra ammunition here. This can be yours if you finish telling us about your rendezvous. While we're still young," she said with a raised eyebrow.

Emily's face broke in to a real smile as she took Sherri's bribe, a giant bag of pistachios. She reached for them as Sherri pulled them away from her.

"These are conditional nuts. You have to earn them," she reminded her.

"That sounds like the name of a song, or a group. 'Conditional Nuts,'" Emily mused. "Girl, don't play with me. Hand over the bag or my lips are sealed and my disposition will be much worse."

Alexis intervened, snatching the bag from Sherri and tossing it to Emily. "Enough of the silly stuff," she said sternly. "It sounds like you and Todd were on your way to something really good. What happened?"

Emily opened the bag and plunged her hand into the salty, fragrant delight that awaited her. "It's the oldest story there is," she said dryly. "He dumped me."

"What do you mean he dumped you?" Sherri asked indignantly.

"I believe it's a real simple concept, the basis of many breakups the world over. Boy and girl meet, boy and girl have spectacular sex, boy tells girl it was a big mistake and it's over. Easy-peasy," Emily said with a distinct sound of bitterness.

"He told you it was a *mistake?*" Alexis, the original ride-or-die girl, looked as if she was ready to head up to Chicago to kick Todd's behind.

Emily had poured another glass of wine, and she took a large swallow before speaking. "We'd been together for a few days. The first day we were like good friends, and the last three we were like good friends with excellent benefits. It was the best time I've ever had. The last morning I woke up and he was sitting on the side of the bed, all dressed. His bags were in the doorway, and he tells me that he'd made a mistake and he was sorry and he hoped I would understand. And he left." She raised her wineglass again, holding it up in a mock toast. "So I've been a little out of sorts lately."

Sherri was stunned into silence, but Alexis certainly wasn't. "What a jerk. Trust me, you're better off without him. Men can be such idiots," she growled. "Any more of that wine?" She picked up the empty bottle and made a face.

"Look in the pantry," Emily said. "Pick anything you want."

"Emily, I really can't believe he did this to you. Do you think he's some kind of sociopath? I mean to be able to turn his feelings on and off like that, it's just not normal," Sherri said. Her face was a mask of concern.

Emily gave a short, harsh laugh. "No, I don't think he's a sociopath, or anything fancy like that. I think he just got a good look at me and decided he couldn't hang with the gangly professor anymore. I've seen the kind of women he dates. I've been up to Chicago several times since the first time I met him, and I usually see him with some real fancy chick. You know, with the perfect hair, the perfect makeup, the perfect body and color coordinated everything. The kind of woman I could never be in a hundred years."

Sherri gave a sharp shake of her head and said, "Don't go there, Em. You are just perfect the way you are. If he's too shallow to know that, it's his loss. He's just not worthy of you."

Emily gave a wan smile. "I'm not so sure about all that, but I appreciate you saying it."

Alexis brought over the bottle of wine she'd selected, along with Emily's fancy corkscrew. She held both items out with a frown. "This is just a suggestion, but you might want to consider a regular ol' opener. Or a bottle with a screw top for your low-class friends like me," she grumbled. Emily deftly opened the bottle and poured some wine into her glass. Alexis smiled gratefully.

"Okay, ladies, raise your glasses. Here's hoping that he's just as miserable as he deserves to be," she said with a steely glint in her eye. "I don't care what he said. He's somewhere right now feeling like the world's biggest moron, which he is."

"I concur," Sherri said.

Emily didn't say a word. She just finished her wine.

Alexis took a few sips and put her glass down. "Just don't get down on yourself, Emmie. I think the chemistry was too much for him," she said slowly. Sherri nodded in agreement, although Emily looked puzzled.

"Chemistry, honey," Sherri emphasized. "This is your field, Emmie. You should understand it better than anyone. Chemistry is the attraction between men and women, and it's a very potent thing. It's what keeps the world turning, so to speak. Yours is really powerful, girl. You turned that man inside out and ran his butt back to Chicago. That's power," she said as she and Alexis did a ladylike high five.

Emily's cheeks were hot, and she decided to ignore them as she cracked more pistachios. She had to smile at the image of Todd fleeing Hilton Head to escape her womanly wiles. *I know that's just sister-love on their part, but I truly hope he's suffering the results of all that so-called chemistry. And I hope he feels as bad as I do.*

It was a miserable, rainy day in Chicago, and it suited Todd just fine. He'd been in a foul mood since he left Hilton Head, and clear, sunny weather was wasted on him. He managed to keep his angst under control when he was working, but when he was alone it was a different story. He was too health-conscious to wallow in alcohol and his personal convictions made drugs totally taboo, but he still needed an outlet for his conflicted emotions. Working out seemed to be his best bet, and he'd been doing so with a vengeance since he returned home. His loft apartment had a corner that held gym equipment that he used when he couldn't get out to run, like today. He was pounding away on his treadmill when his brother Jason came into the loft.

"Did I invite you here? Because unexpected is uninvited," Todd growled.

"If you'd answer your phone or return a call I wouldn't have to invade your privacy," Jason replied. "But since you've put up this huge wall around yourself lately, this was my only recourse."

"Why don't you just recourse yourself on out of

here?" Todd slowed the treadmill down to a walk and wiped his face with the towel that was slung over his shoulder.

Jason didn't seem to react to his brother's rudeness. In fact, he looked a tiny bit amused. He went over to the refrigerator to see if there was anything worth eating and shook his head when he saw nothing but some withered fruit and takeout containers. "There's something very familiar and ironic about this situation," he mused.

Todd got off the treadmill and went to the kitchen area to get a big glass of water from the water cooler. "What are you talking about?"

"It wasn't too long ago that you were coming to my place, uninvited I might add, to needle me about the state of my love life. And now I get to do the same thing to you," Jason said with a grin.

Todd's face darkened with anger, and he was about to tear into his brother when Jason held up both hands. "Look, man, I'm concerned about you. I'm not trying to yank your chain for the fun of it. You went on vacation to get some rest because you were stressed out and tired. You come back from vacation looking like hell and evil as a black snake. I know you well enough to know that something happened between then and now, and you need to talk about it."

"No, I don't. There's nothing to talk about," Todd said stubbornly. "Why don't you go on back to your happy home and mind your own damned business?"

Jason ignored him as he went over to the super-size sofa and sat down, picking up the remote and turning on the giant flat-screen. "I'm not going anywhere until we talk, because your bad mood is affecting my happy home. I'm worried about you, and what worries me worries my wife. And I'm not having her upset over anything if I can help it. Especially not now. You're going to be an uncle again."

Todd's whole demeanor changed. "Seriously? That's great news! When did you find out?"

Jason looked at him sardonically. "Two weeks after you got back from Hilton Head. Which you would have known if you hadn't tried to drop off the grid to sulk."

Todd looked slightly abashed. "Yeah, you're right. Let me take a quick shower while you order some takeout. I guess I need to get a few things off my chest."

In a short while, the two men were sitting at the counter that divided the kitchen area from the rest of the loft, eating Thai food while Todd filled Jason in on why he'd been acting like an ass for weeks.

"So after the initial shock of finding out that Emily and I were sharing the house, everything was great. She's an amazing woman, Jason. She's brilliant, for one thing. She's also funny, athletic, totally beautiful and totally natural. Emily is like light-years away from any of the women I've been dating. When we were together it was like nothing I've ever had with a woman before. That's why I knew I'd screwed everything up."

Jason looked blank for a moment. "I get it. You messed up because you weren't treating her like she was special. You felt like you needed to start over and do it right," he said.

"Exactly," Todd replied. "You know, I used to dog you about your revolving bimbettes, but that's what I've been doing, too. You think it might be genetic?"

They both laughed. "I'm serious, man. I used to stay on your case about that endless parade of gorgeous women that trailed after you," Todd said, "and I started doing the same damn thing. Some of these women are total predators, man. They come after a guy with no shame whatsoever. They set their sights on somebody and come charging. And it's not like they're looking to get married. They just want a lot of sex and no commitment. A lot of them bring their own condoms," he said, shaking his head.

"All women aren't that way," Jason reminded him.

"Of course they aren't. I'm not that stupid. But the women I've been hanging out with definitely are. No strings, no commitments, they just want a good time. So I've apparently forgotten everything I ever knew about how to treat a lady. I should have been trying to get to know Emily instead of hopping in the bed with her. I should have been doing the candy, flowers and long walks thing, but instead I was all over her," he said glumly.

"So what did you do about that?"

"I did the right thing. I told her that I'd made a huge mistake and I wished I'd handled things differently."

Jason raised both brows. "Okay, so you manned up. There's nothing wrong with owning up to your errors and getting a fresh start. How's that working for you?"

"Not too well. If I call her cell, it goes straight to voice mail. If I call her at work, she's in a lecture or a lab or something. If I call her at home, it goes to voice mail. I've sent plants, I've emailed; I've done everything but drive to Columbia to camp on her doorstep." He looked both angry and miserable. "This is real messed up, Jason. I finally meet the perfect woman and fall in love, and she drops me like a hot rock and I have no idea why."

"Man, you sound like you're about seventeen," Jason muttered. In a normal tone of voice, he went on. "But since I went through the same thing with my lovely wife and you were a real stand-up brother while I was losing my natural mind, I'm going to help you out."

Todd looked slightly intrigued but doubtful. "How?"

"I know where Emily is going to be and when. That is, if you think seeing her face-to-face would be of benefit to you."

Todd answered him in very loud and profane terms, but he was looking much more cheerful as he did.

Chapter 9

Emily drove to work with a smile on her face for the first time in weeks. She was feeling a lot better after her friends ambushed her. Their intervention had lifted some of the weight of the depression she'd been unsuccessfully trying to ignore since the end of her disastrous vacation. Now instead of feeling angry, bitter and gullible all day long, she felt bitter when she woke up and gullible before she went to bed. That left her a whole day in between to feel like a normal person, a person who hadn't been duped in the worst possible way. Pretty soon she would be feeling better in the mornings. Then she'd be feeling better at bedtime, and then she'd be done with the whole thing.

She parked her Mini Cooper in the faculty lot and walked to her building to get ready for her early class. One thing hadn't changed: her love for her work. The fact that she'd let her guard down and gotten her heart smashed to atoms wasn't going to ruin her career. She was actually smiling when she entered the science building. Exchanging greetings with her fellow professors and various students lifted her spirits even more, until she got to her office and found yet another huge potted plant awaiting her. She didn't bother to look at the card; she knew the name of the sender perfectly well.

She put her leather tote bag in its usual place and turned on her computer, talking to the department administrator as she did so. "Jessy, do you want another plant? If you do, please feel free to take this one."

Jessy was an older woman who handled the biochemistry department's administrative duties with amazing efficiency. She came into Emily's office with a wry smile on her face. "I'll just put it out here with the others. One of these days you're going to have to give that poor young man a break. He must be going broke sending all these pretty plants."

Emily gave her a half smile that was almost diabolical. "Good. I'm off to class," she said cheerfully.

Jessy shook her head as Emily took off at her usual fast pace. "You can run but you can't hide. One of these days that young man is going to catch you. I hope I'm there to see it," she said mostly to herself.

Emily was so busy that she didn't get a chance to check her messages until midafternoon. She was pleased to see that her mother had called. Ever since Lucie Porter retired from her career in nursing, she'd been traveling. So much that Emily actually saw less of her mother than when she'd been a busy working woman. Emily returned the call and smiled when she heard her mother's voice.

"I didn't know you were home. I thought you were still in Paris."

"I am still in Paris, dear. I'm calling because my travel plans have changed. I was coming home next week, but I've changed my mind. I talked to Ayanna last night and she had a wonderful idea. Instead of coming back to Columbia, I'm going to Chicago for a couple of weeks. I miss my grandbabies and I want to spend some time with them. And Ayanna wants to give you a big birthday party over the Thanksgiving weekend, so you have to come too. The timing is perfect because it coincides with your break at the university. Doesn't that sound like fun?"

As usual, Lucie's good mood was infectious. It was very difficult to be down in the dumps around her. Emily laughed at her enthusiasm. "Mom, slow down! You're talking so fast I can barely keep up. But, yes, it sounds like a plan. I'll just come to Chicago, then. It'll be wonderful to see everybody, but I don't need to have a birthday party. Tell Ayanna not to worry about it."

"Absolutely not! She's looking forward to it, and she's already started planning it."

Quite naturally, Lucie had the last word. She wasn't bossy, but she was persuasive and, as she freely admitted, she liked having her own way. Her daughters had no problem indulging her because she was so sweet. They talked a bit more and when the call ended, Emily was smiling. There was a time when she and Ayanna hadn't been close at all. Ayanna had told Emily about her funky attitude, and after a while Emily had conceded that her older sister was right. It had cleared the air and started them on a path to a much better relationship. She was also much closer to her mother now. She was really looking forward to going to Chicago. It wasn't until she was walking out to her car that she remembered something vital. She remembered just why going anywhere near the Windy City was a totally bad idea.

Sherri opened the door to her condo, looking concerned. "Come on in here, Em. You sounded a little stressed on the phone." She gave Emily a quick hug and patted her on the back before turning to lead the way into the living room. Her condo was nicely decorated in earth tones with pops of bright orange and coral. There were cheerful African and Caribbean prints on the walls, as well as big healthy green plants.

Emily walked into the living room, where she was greeted with great gusto by Sherri's adorable and very precocious five-year-old daughter, Sydney. "Hi, Auntie Emily! I haven't seen you in a long time," she said. She was the image of her mother. She looked just as Sherri had as a child, right down to the long pigtails and the round eyeglasses that slid down to the tip of her nose.

Emily picked her up and gave her a big kiss on the cheek. "It hasn't been that long has it?"

Sydney nodded her head vigorously. "It's been a long, long time. Are you going to have dinner with us?"

Emily was about to say no when Sherri interrupted. "Yes, she is. So why don't you go take off your school clothes and wash your hands so you can help me set the table?"

"Okay!" Sydney wiggled down from Emily's arms and dashed off to her bedroom.

"Come on in the kitchen and we'll talk. We're just having leftovers, so don't act like this is an imposition. What's up?"

Emily sat on a stool by the counter that served

as a breakfast bar and room divider. "I talked to my mom today. She wanted to tell me her travel plans. She's going to Chicago for a couple of weeks, and I'm supposed to meet her up there because Ayanna wants to give me a birthday party. And I said of course I'd come, sure no problem." She crossed her arms on the counter and propped her head up with one hand.

Sherri was making a salad and looked up when Emily stopped talking. "Why so glum? It'll be a great time."

"Where does Todd live, Sherri?" Emily stared at her friend, waiting for the penny to drop.

"What do you mean, where does he live? He lives in… Oh, I get it. Hmm."

"Took you long enough," Emily said grumpily. "I'll be walking into the lair of the beast. I'll see him up there, there's no question about it. My sister is married to Johnny Phillips. Johnny Phillips's sister Billie is married to Todd's brother, and they're all like best friends. We're just one big happy freakin' family. There is no way I could be in Chicago for any amount of time and not run into him."

Sherri had finished tossing the salad and put the bowl on the counter. "Good. You *should* run into him. It's just what you need to do. You need to show up looking fabulous and rub his nose in it. That way you'll be free of him and you can move on, leaving him to wallow in his own misery," she said firmly.

Emily looked at Sherri as if birds were flying out of her ears. "Are you feeling okay? This is me we're talking about, Sherri. I don't do gorgeous. I don't have the gorgeous gene. I do smart. That's my whole thing, girlfriend."

Sherri ignored her while she began heating the meat loaf and macaroni and cheese that she'd referred to as just leftovers. "Smart and gorgeous aren't mutually exclusive. All you need is a few minor adjustments to your stubborn mind-set and a couple of fairy godmothers, and you'll be fine."

Before Emily could demand to know what she meant, the doorbell rang. "And here's our other godmother, right on schedule. Can you see what Sydney is doing and help her set the table while I answer the door? Thanks, Em," she said breezily as she left the kitchen.

Emily was too bemused to do anything but follow Sherri's orders. She went in search of Sydney, who had changed out of her school uniform and into play clothes. She was standing on a little stool washing her hands, like the obedient child she was. "C'mon, chick, we're going to set the table."

As they came down the hall they heard Alexis's voice, and Sydney ran to greet her while Emily took a deep breath. She had a feeling she was going to be talked into something she wasn't going to like. When she saw the gloating smiles on her friends' faces, she gave a deep sigh and prepared to face the inevitable. They most assuredly had big plans for her, and she might as well save herself from long hours of argument and get with the program.

Chapter 10

Emily's prediction proved to be absolutely correct. She didn't understand quite how they did it, but Alexis and Sherri had convinced her that she was overdue for a new look. They were kind enough not to use the word "makeover," but that's what it amounted to. That's why she was sitting in Alexis's styling chair on a Sunday. They had gone to the early service at church, and Sydney was spending the afternoon with her grandmother. Emily had so much hair that Alexis wanted to do her on a day when she didn't have any other clients. She was glad about that, because she would have chickened out if a lot of people were in the salon.

Now, since it was just her and Sherri and Alexis, she didn't mind sitting in the styling chair with a cape tied around her neck.

She'd never been in the salon for longer than a few minutes, and she was most impressed. It was a clean, uncluttered place with a robin's egg blue and chocolate-brown color scheme that was soothing and chic. There were a lot of stations for other stylists, as well as a section for manicures and pedicures and other beauty services that Emily had never had. She hadn't even heard of most of them. Alexis told her to take the elastic off her hair and Emily did so, then she laughed at Alexis's reaction.

"Girl, this is a whole lotta hair," Alexis said. "You've got enough for three people."

"Yeah, I do. I've never had it cut, except for when you used to trim the ends every so often. And as you know, I've never had a perm or had it pressed or anything. All I ever did was wash it and braid it up to get it out of the way," Emily admitted. In a burst of frankness, she said, "It just seemed kind of pointless. I was never going to look as good as my sisters, so why bother. Ouch!" She turned around to stare at Alexis. "You pulled my hair!"

"Yes I did," Alexis said without a hint of remorse. "This is Emily time. This is when you look forward with positivity and joy. We are not spending any time looking back with negativity and anger, you got that?"

Emily nodded and smiled. It was so good to have girlfriends who were completely and totally on her side. Every woman needed some friends who "had her back," as Alexis and Sherri did hers. "Yes, Earth Mother, I got it."

"All right, then, let's get to work. *Namaste.*" Alexis loved having the last word. "And by the way, you're still not getting a perm. Permanent waves make the hair curlier. Relaxers are what make the hair straighter. I wish people wouldn't use those terms interchangeably," she grumbled as she combed through Emily's hair.

"I'm putting myself totally in your hands, Alexis. You can dye it, fry it, snip it or clip it, whatever you want. I do have one question. Can my hair be donated to Locks of Love?"

Alexis gave her a big smile. "Yes, it most certainly can. I'm not going to cut it too short. I'm going to cut it to right below your shoulders. That's plenty of hair to donate, and you'll still have a lot to play with."

It sounded fine to Emily, and she sat patiently while Alexis took a load off her head. She really felt as if a weight was gone, and she told Alexis so.

"Just wait until I relax it," she replied. "You'll feel even lighter."

Remembering how much Todd claimed to dislike relaxers, Emily gave her reflection a wicked little smile. She couldn't wait to get it done. A thought occurred to her, and she asked Alexis if she was going to show her how to put on makeup.

"Of course! Your skin is so pretty you won't need much, but I'm going to shape your eyebrows first."

Emily stared in the mirror again and ran her finger over one of her brows. They weren't bushy, but they didn't look sleek and sexy like the ones on Alexis and Sherri. She resigned herself to the inevitable, but she had another question. "Does it hurt?"

"No more than childbirth," Sherri said with a grin.

Emily braced herself and clutched the arms of the styling chair, preparing herself for the worst. Alexis rolled her eyes and leaned in for the attack. She held the skin taut and went to work.

"Just tell me when you're going to start," Emily whined.

"I'm done, you big sissy. It only hurts if you don't know what you're doing," Alexis said as she changed brows.

"Wow." She tried to look in the mirror, but Alexis blocked her. "Let me see how it looks," Emily said.

"You can't see anything until I'm all done. I want you to get the total effect."

"That's so not fair," Emily protested. "You know I have immediate gratification syndrome. I want to see it in progress."

"Nope. Just sit there and be patient while I work my magic. And please remember that I have some very hot curling irons here. You wouldn't want to get a little burn, would you?"

Sherri looked up from the catalogs she'd been perusing. "Be patient, Em. You know she means it," she said. "How do you think she keeps her clients in line?"

All three women laughed, but Emily resolved to sit quietly through the whole process, especially since Alexis was doing this solely from the goodness of her heart. She had absolutely refused any kind of payment, which made Emily treasure her friend even more. It really didn't take as long as Emily had anticipated. In a few hours her hair had been cut, relaxed and styled, her eyebrows had been shaped and Alexis had put on a light application of makeup. Sherri and Alexis were very pleased with the results.

"Okay, close your eyes. I'm turning you around," Alexis said.

Emily did so at once, her hands tightly clasped together. She felt the chair moving and heard Alexis tell her to take a look. Her eyes popped open and she stared at the woman in the mirror. Her reflection was so unfamiliar that she half turned to see who was standing behind her. She realized what she was doing and turned back to view her new look. Emily was stunned.

"I look…good," she said slowly.

Sherri patted her shoulder. "You are beautiful, honey. You look like you from the inside out."

"I look like my mom." For the first time in her life she saw the resemblance to her gorgeous mother. Her hair was silky and shiny, parted on one side with a deep wave that highlighted her eyes. Her eyebrows were still thick, but cleanly shaped. The effect was so dramatic that it drew attention to her big eyes, framed by long eyelashes. Bronze highlighter and soft plum blush brought out her cheekbones, and a nude lip gloss showed off the shape of her lips. Emily was stunned. "I really look nice," she said softly. She got a little teary-eyed, which caused Alexis to thrust a tissue at her.

"That mascara is good, but it's not waterproof. And you don't look nice, girl. You look fabulous!"

Emily smiled widely. "I do, don't I?" She stood and hugged Alexis tight, then Sherri. "You know what I feel like?"

"A million bucks," Sherri said.

"A new woman," Alexis guessed.

"Oh, absolutely. I feel brand-new and I feel like

ten million bucks. But I really feel like shopping," Emily said as she turned her head from side to side. "I need new clothes. Lots of them."

Sherri rubbed her hands together gleefully. "Okay, it's time for me to work my magic. Ladies, let's hit the mall!"

Two weeks later, Emily was leaning back into her rather uncomfortable seat on the plane that was taking her to Chicago. She'd made the trip many times since Ayanna had moved to Illinois, but this was going to be a totally different experience. Even the most mundane aspects of this trip were foreign to her. For the first time ever, Emily had to pay a hefty fee for having overweight luggage. She'd always been indifferent to her attire and she could roll everything up into a small suitcase. If her clothes got wrinkled, she didn't care because clothing was functional, not decorative, as far as she was concerned. Those days were totally over. Now her luggage was carefully packed and loaded with fashionable outfits and accessories.

She couldn't have cared less about the extra fees. It was worth it, as a matter of fact, because it was her time to shine. Her mother and her sister would be tickled about the new Emily, but she couldn't wait until she bumped into Todd Wainwright. Emily was going to show him what a huge mistake he'd made by dumping her so crudely. She couldn't wait to see the look on his face when they encountered each other again. She could run into Todd in the airport and it wouldn't make any difference to her—she was more than ready. There was a time when she'd wear old jeans and a sweatshirt to travel in, but not anymore. She was wearing black skinny jeans with a bright red turtleneck sweater and some really sexy black over-the-knee boots with a black wool peacoat. No more flying slob for her.

Emily looked fantastic and she knew it, which is a great confidence builder for any woman, even one as brilliant and accomplished as she was. Going to work after her haircut and shopping spree was gratifying, to say the least. Reactions ranged from disbelief to open awe to confusion. Two of her colleagues didn't recognize her. Jessy, the department administrator, was delighted with the changes to Emily's appearance and told her so.

"Now that's the real you," she said, beaming. "I could never figure out why you wanted to hide behind clothes that were all baggy and why you never let anyone see how pretty you are. And all it took was a little haircut and some clothes that fit you right. Now people can see that great figure of yours and those pretty legs, too."

Emily gave the older woman a smile and a cheeky wink, which made both of them laugh. She was getting used to the extra attention, and it was rather pleasant. A few weeks ago it seemed that attention to one's appearance was the height of social stupidity, something that indicated the paucity of true intellect in this society. But it was hard to apply that line of thought when fellow scholars with many advanced degrees were smiling at her with approval. And it was impossible to deny that she was feeling more confident as a result of a simple change in her mode of dress and style of her hair. She had even impressed those above her, as she found out when having lunch with the university provost.

Dr. Gavin Awerbuch had been at the university much longer than Emily, which was saying something because she'd started so young and excelled so fast. He'd been a mentor to her for a long time, and he was someone she could count on for good advice and counsel. They met off-campus at a nice restaurant that was frequented by faculty and students alike. He was one of her favorite people. He had a wild head of curly hair, a short beard, and he always wore unusual eyeglasses. This pair looked like something H. G. Wells would have worn, with oddly shaped wire frames that gave him the air of a keen-eyed mad scientist.

After a delicious seafood lunch and chitchat, Dr. A., as she called him when they were alone, got down to business.

"Emily, do you want my job?"

She started to laugh, but she could see he was quite serious. "No, I don't. You're not thinking of retiring, are you? You're too young for that," she said with concern on her face and in her voice.

"Thanks for saying that. My kids make me feel like an antique some of the time. Teenagers can do that," he said with a grin. "The reason I bring it up is because we don't know what to do with you. You're so young, yet so accomplished that the only way for you to go is up, and right now there's no place to put you. A lateral move would be ridiculous, and there's no one for you to replace."

"Is that a bad thing?"

"In a way yes, and in other ways, of course not," he assured her. "You've been responsible for recruiting and developing some of the finest scientific minds we've acquired in the last decade. But you've also been instrumental in us losing them."

Emily had to stifle a gasp as she tried not to choke on her iced tea. She was struggling to answer this cryptic statement when he hastened to reassure her.

"It's nothing personal, Emmie. Everyone loves you and you do a superlative job in everything that you do. You are the kind of professor, department head and colleague that every university prays for, trust me. But," he added, raising his index finger, "you are an impossible act to follow. The scholars you develop have to leave here in order to advance.

You train your people brilliantly, you stimulate their intellectual curiosity, you spur them to aspire to greatness, and just when they are primed to be of real use to us, they have to take everything you've given them and leave our gates because there is no place for them to go. In order for them to spread their academic wings they've got to fly away from the nest, which is, from the standpoint of the board both a blessing and a curse. A blessing because your name and reputation attract more of the same kind of eager scholars, and a curse because we want to keep them all," he said, gesturing with both hands. "So, my dear Emily, my question is, what do you plan to do with the rest of your life? You've already accomplished more than many academics do in a lifetime, and you're barely thirty. What's next for you?"

Emily stared out the window for a long moment, watching the traffic go by. For once she had no answer, nothing that she could say that would make any sense. She finally looked into Dr. A.'s dark, clever eyes and told him the truth. "I have absolutely no idea. Just none."

"Don't look so stricken, Emily. I put it badly," he apologized. "I was thinking out loud, which is always a bad idea. Since I'm treating, how about a huge slab of that pecan pie? You could use a nice sugar rush for the afternoon."

"That sounds like a great idea." Emily tried to

put a big smile on her face, but it would be a while before she could process the information she'd just been given. Thank God she was going on vacation next week. The long plane ride would give her plenty of time to think about what Dr. A. had just shared with her.

Emily could hear the sound of the jet going into a descent. It would be landing soon, but there would be no one to meet her, per her request. People didn't go to the mass confusion that was O'Hare Airport with joy in their hearts, and she wasn't about to drag her sister or brother-in-law out there when she was perfectly capable of getting to their house by herself. There were plenty of limos and cabs and other means of transportation available; she'd get there just fine. She was jolted out of her thoughts when the man sitting next to her asked if she needed a lift from the airport. He was a very handsome man named Jared and they had chatted almost the entire flight.

"Is someone meeting you, or would you like a ride into the city?" he asked. He had the most arresting gray eyes and a deep cleft in his chin. With his blond hair and rugged build, he rather resembled Alexander Skarsgard, the actor who played her favorite vampire on *True Blood*.

She turned to face him, her head still inclined on the headrest. "Jared, that's nice of you, but I'll get a cab. My family wanted to pick me up, but I think coming to almost any airport is cruel and unusual punishment."

He had a devastating smile, one that lit up his whole face. She was admiring it while he answered.

"You are a woman of great decency and common sense. And you probably wouldn't be comfortable letting a stranger take you anywhere. I don't blame you. I wouldn't be too happy if my sister accepted a ride with some bum she met on a plane."

His smile made the corners of his eyes crinkle in a very sexy way, and Emily smiled back. "You don't come across as a bum to me, and I'm a fairly good judge of character," she said.

"At least let me accompany you to the baggage claim and make sure you get a cab. And then maybe you'll be inclined to let me take you to lunch while we're here in Chicago."

Emily hesitated a moment before saying "Maybe I will." It was noncommittal, but she said it with a smile. He was handsome and charming, but he didn't overdo it with the charm. He had a good sense of humor, which everyone needed when flying commercial. Air travel used to be fun and fast and now it was neither, but on this flight Emily didn't get impatient and irascible the way she usually did. By mutual agreement, she and Jared didn't try to hurry off the crowded plane. They enjoyed talking to each other until the plane was almost empty. He insisted on getting her carry-on bag and rolling it down the jetway with his own bag. Emily couldn't ever recall having a man do something like that for her since her father died. He was the last man who'd treated her like a lady. Her cheeks flushed as she realized that Jared was the first man she'd ever allowed to treat her with deference, other than Todd.

Jared was a real sweet guy, Emily decided as they reached the baggage claim. The fact that the luggage from their plane hadn't reached the carousel yet didn't bother him in the least. To her surprise, it didn't stress her out either, although it would have made her crazy in the past. She'd have been mentally composing the scathing letter she was going to send to the airline and growling at everyone who got within five feet of her. Now she was just enjoying talking to Jared, who made sure that they exchanged cell phone numbers. Her bags would show up eventually, and there was no point in getting bent out of shape about it. Sure enough, the bags came out and Jared again showed what a gentleman he was by hauling the large, heavy bag off the carousel. Then he made sure she got into a cab. He did everything with such aplomb and efficiency that Emily totally missed the fact that someone had come to meet her after all. She was so engrossed with Jared that she missed Todd Wainwright completely.

Chapter 11

Emily raised her hand to ring Ayanna's doorbell, but the door flew open before she could make contact. Lucie was standing in the doorway with a huge smile on her face.

"Hey, Mom," Emily said. "Were you standing here waiting for me?"

"Yes, I was! Oh, goodness, look at you," Lucie said as she grabbed her for a big hug. "You look just wonderful, sweetie. Come on in here," she urged.

The cabdriver was standing behind her with her bags, much to her mother's amusement. After he left, her mother told her that most cabdrivers wouldn't bring the luggage to the door.

"They usually leave it on the curb," she said dryly. "But I can see why he went out of his way for you. You dazzled him, girl."

By now Ayanna had come into the foyer with a smile on her face. "Is that my little sister?" she said teasingly. Her smile got bigger as she got a good look at Emily. "Oh, snap! You are too fabulous, baby girl. Take off that coat and turn around so I can see your hair."

Emily promptly executed a graceful turn, which brought applause from her family. The ladies were joined by Ayanna's handsome and devoted husband, who took a long look at his sister-in-law and smiled broadly before giving her a big hug and a kiss on the cheek. "You are a beautiful woman, Emily. You're lookin' good, sis," he said. "Let me take those bags upstairs for you."

They went into the huge living room of the big brick house that Johnny and Ayanna had restored. The extended family lived pretty close to each other in turn-of-the-century homes that had been remodeled, restored and put into mint condition. Johnny had two sisters, one who was married to a contractor and one who was a contractor, so naturally, refurbishing was in their blood, so to speak. Ayanna's house hadn't needed much work, just lots of painting and furnishing. Thanks to her creative decorating, Ayanna's home was warm and cozy, despite the big rooms and high ceilings.

"Are you hungry? We'll be eating soon," Lucie said.

"Something smells really good," Emily said, sniffing the air.

"You're in for a treat," Lucie assured her. "Johnny decided to cook tonight."

"That sounds great, but before I eat, I want to see my nieces. Where are Madison and Lindsey?"

Ayanna went to the doorway and beckoned her. "I was just about to get them. Come on upstairs. You won't believe how big they are."

Emily was truly amazed at the sight of the two-year-old twins. They still had a little of that sweet baby chubbiness, but they were much taller. They had the same golden-brown skin as Emily and Ayanna, with curly black hair and big black eyes. They even had Emily's dimples. The little girls remembered her, calling her Auntie Emmie and giving her lots of kisses. Her throat got a little tight for some reason. *Just because I haven't seen them in so long,* she thought as she hugged them both.

After she freshened up, she and Ayanna each took a twin and went downstairs to the dining room, where the table was already set and her nephews, Alex and Cameron, were pouring ice water and placing a big bowl of salad on the table. They'd just come home from practice for the academic Olympics for their high school and had been immediately put to work. Their eyes lit up and Emily was bombarded with hugs. Billie Wain-wright was also there with her husband, Jason, Todd's older brother. All in all it was quite a gathering. The only ones missing were Billie's charming sister Dakota and her husband, Nick Hunter. Dakota and Nick were at home because one of their little ones was sick, but they would see plenty of them soon. The elder Phillipses, Johnny's parents, were in town and that meant more festivity. It was like a big extended family because all the couples were close friends as well as being in-laws, in some cases. At one time Emily felt like the odd person out in the face of all this wedded bliss, but she'd gotten past all of that because everyone made her feel welcome.

Finally, everyone was seated around the table, grace was said and dinner, which consisted of Johnny's excellent spaghetti and his homemade bread, was served. Emily ate until she was stuffed, enjoying the laughter and easy conversation. She usually dined alone, so this much family was a welcome change. She got up to help with the dishes, but Alex and Cameron insisted that it was their job. After the delicious meal, they all went into the family room, which was actually the former basement of the house. It had been completely finished, so it was just as nice as the rest of the house. She was so busy laughing and talking and playing with her nieces that she didn't hear the doorbell ring, but she did recognize the deep voice that was coming toward the stairs. It was Todd, talking to Johnny, who'd opened the door for him.

"I know you said she would get here on her own, but I went to the airport to pick Emily up and she wasn't there. She must have caught a later flight. Did she call you?" His voice was just as mellow and sexy as she remembered, and Emily was trying not to react to it.

Todd waved and gave a general hello to everyone in the room. He glanced at Emily for the briefest of seconds before turning his whole attention to Johnny, who was looking amused. Suddenly Todd's face froze into a strange expression, and he turned back to Emily. His eyes widened and he scanned her from the top of her head to the soles of her boots and then back again. He opened his mouth to speak, closed it and then opened it again, this time speaking directly to Emily. "My God, what did you do to yourself?" It was impossible, of course, but Emily could have sworn she heard the chirping of crickets in the sudden silence that descended on the room.

Todd felt like a total fool, but he couldn't pull his foot out of his mouth. It was too late for that, he surmised as he looked at the identical expressions on the faces of the women. Emily looked at him as though he was a stranger, one she didn't want to get to know. It was a surreal moment, because she looked like a stranger to him, too, but there was something all too familiar and seductive about her. Ayanna looked at him then at Emily, and he could just about tell the exact moment when she figured out the subtext of his behavior.

"Mom, can you help me get my little ladies upstairs for a nice bath?" Ayanna sounded diplomatic and neutral, but she gave Todd a definite side eye as she took Lindsey from Emily and handed her to Lucie. She put Madison on her hip and was about to leave the room when Billie said she was coming, too. Her son, Jason Jr., was almost three and was asleep on her shoulder. She tried to stand up, but Jason took the sleep-heavy toddler from her arms and helped her stand while he gave Todd a cold stare.

The exodus took almost no time. There was no one left in the family room but Johnny, Emily and Todd. Todd expelled a deep breath and prepared himself for a mean mugging from Johnny. Emily was Johnny's sister-in-law, and Todd knew he was on thin ice right about now. Johnny was very protective of every member of his family, including his wife's sister. But before anything could be said by Johnny or done to Todd, Ayanna called her husband, and he left the room so he could see what she needed. He did look back at Todd and point his index finger at him as if it was a pistol. Now it was just him and Emily, and he was trying to think of something clever and conciliatory to say to her.

Emily was apparently not at a loss for words. She rose to her feet quite gracefully and stared at him with little liking as she crossed her arms under her breasts. She looked like a different person, yet she looked totally familiar at the same time. Her hair was much shorter and was really glossy and sexy-looking. He couldn't tell if she was wearing makeup or not, but her lips were lush and inviting and her eyes were big and smoky. She smelled good, too. There was something totally compelling about her, but he couldn't say whether or not it was a good thing. He was totally confused by her new appearance, but captivated at the same time. Something was lurking in the back of his mind, but it wasn't surfacing. Her cell phone buzzed and she pulled it out of her pocket. She glanced at the caller ID and looked extremely pleased before she answered it.

"Hello, Jared! I'm so glad you called," she said happily.

It was the way she pushed her thick, heavy hair out of the way to position the phone that finally clicked in his head. He had seen her at the airport, after all. He distinctly recalled seeing a tall, pretty woman who had a tall blond guy hanging all over her. The man was obviously flirting with her and she was flirting back. Todd hadn't recognized Emily at all. Now that all the pieces had fallen into place, Todd was furious. And he was also jealous, if he was going to be honest with himself. He couldn't take his eyes off her. She was just babbling away on her damned cell phone as if he wasn't even in the room. She was probably talking to the overgrown blond right now.

"Lunch sounds wonderful, Jared," she said. "I'd love to."

By the time she finally ended the call, Todd felt as if his head was going to blow up. Emily went right back to looking at him as if he was a very low form of life, while he tried to say something that would get him out of the giant hole he'd dug for himself.

"So how are you doing?" he asked gruffly.

Emily raised one of her newly shaped eyebrows before answering. "I'm just fine, Todd. A better question would be how *you're* doing, because you don't seem to be yourself tonight," she said in a cool, calm voice he had trouble recognizing as hers. She flicked her hair behind her ear, waiting for him to answer. She looked like a gorgeous alien; an exotic feminine life-form he'd never encountered before.

"What in the hell did you do to yourself?" The words were out of his mouth before he could stop them. *Whomp, Whomp.*

* * *

"You've lost your mind," Emily said incredulously. "I knew you were slightly untrustworthy, inconsiderate and trampy, but I always thought you were sane. I haven't seen you for months, and all you can do is ask me what I've done to myself? I was so damned homely that only major plastic surgery would improve me, is that what I'm hearing?"

"No, that's not what I'm saying at all. You were perfect just the way you were. Why did you have to go and do all of this?" he asked, gesturing with his hand as he spoke.

"I was so perfect so you told me we'd made a big mistake and you ran out of the house so fast you left skid marks on the floor," she said scornfully. "And now you're—I don't know what you are. Upset because you don't like my new hairstyle?"

"No, that's not it. You're taking this all wrong," Todd replied hastily.

"You got through medical school with that brain? No wonder the health care system is in such bad shape. Let me explain something to you, Todd. When a woman has on a new outfit, or does something different to her hair, 'what the hell did you do to yourself' is not considered a compliment. In any culture. I don't know why you've decided to insult me, but you're doing a bang-up job," she said hotly.

Todd knew he'd put his foot in his mouth again, but he kept right on like an out-of-control battering ram. "I'm not trying to insult you. I'm concerned about you," he said. It seemed like a good start to him, but Emily cut him off again.

"Really, Todd? Wow, you're a real friend to look out for my better interests. But why are you so concerned? Are you under the impression that I'm suddenly incapable of taking care of myself?"

She looked so striking that for a moment Todd finally understood why men said ignorant things like "you're beautiful when you're angry." He went the other way, though, which was just as ignorant. "I don't think you know what you're doing, Emily. I know you're as smart as Einstein and you have all kinds of degrees, but I don't think you have a lot of experience in other things," he said. Emily's mouth opened as he forged ahead to make his point.

"Look, I saw you at the airport with that big blond guy. He was all over you, and you don't know him from a can of paint. He could be a serial killer for all you know, and you're letting him hang all over you. That's why I'm concerned," he added piously.

If her eyes could have shot lightning, he would've fried from the look on her face. Suddenly her expression changed and she got the real calm look that's ultimately more dangerous. "His name is Jared Van Buren and he owns five restaurants, six if you count the one he's opening in Columbia. His mother is on the board of the hospital where you work and his father is the chief of staff. I'm sure that if you want more information on Jared, Dr. Van Buren will be more than happy to supply it," she said in the quiet voice of a woman who knows she's got the upper hand.

"How do you know he didn't make up all this crap?"

"Look him up on Google if you don't believe me. I dare you."

While they'd been arguing, they had unconsciously gotten closer to each other, and now they were close enough for Todd to reach out and pull her into his arms for a long, scorching kiss. As soon as their mouths touched he was on fire, the same blaze that had consumed him when they were together on Hilton Head. His tongue teased her soft, full lips until she yielded to him. His hands were on her waist and he pulled her even closer, but he stopped cold when his pager went off.

"I'm on call tonight." He let go of Emily so abruptly she stumbled, but he didn't notice. He was walking to the door with his cell phone clamped to his ear while Emily glared at him. Todd ended the call and turned to say goodbye.

"We have a lot to talk about. I'll call you tomorrow, okay?"

He was out the door before Emily could say a word.

Chapter 12

Emily was full of mixed emotions after Todd left the house. She was adult enough to pretend that everything was okay until the guests left and everyone had gone to bed, but she was plenty salty. She didn't like what Todd had said to her. She was pissed that he'd had the gall to bring up Jared, and she was mad that he had to leave before they could finish arguing. And she was also furiously angry that he'd kissed her, because his lips had lit her up like a blazing fire on a cold night. After he told her that he'd made a mistake in sleeping with her, he had the unmitigated gall to put his hands on her as if they belonged there. And her traitorous body had no better sense than to respond. She, in the words of her dearly loved late grandmother, didn't know whether to wind her ass or scratch her watch.

She took a hot shower and put on a pretty purple nightdress. It was part of the Sherri and Alexis shopping spree, and normally it made her feel happy and sexy. It wasn't working for her tonight. She had parted her hair and wrapped it the way Alexis had taught her, and she was about to tie a silk scarf over it when she heard a soft tap on the door. It was Ayanna.

"Just wanted to make sure you had everything you needed," she said, sitting on the side of the big bed. "And I hope Todd didn't upset you. By the way, I'm loving that gown. Where did you get it?"

"Sherri took me shopping after Alexis did my hair." Emily twirled around to show off the silky perfection of the gown with its spaghetti straps and lace bodice. "Look at the other stuff she helped me pick out." She opened the closet door and pulled open the dresser drawers to show off her new clothes.

Ayanna admired the outfits with envy in her voice. "Girl, these things are gorgeous! If I wasn't so short I'd make off with that black pencil skirt. And the cashmere sweater that goes with it. And that red dress! You do have good taste."

"No, I have a *friend* with good taste," Emily

corrected her. "And she knows where to shop, too. We wore T.J. Maxx out!"

Ayanna laughed and offered her hand for a fist bump. "I love that place. We'll have to go there while you're here." She was holding a silk blouse up to her chest and admiring it in the mirror. "So what brought this about, sister? I mean the big change. You look fabulous, just wonderful," she said hastily. "But what was the impetus for the big reveal?"

"Reveal?" Emily looked puzzled.

"Yes, a *reveal*," Ayanna said emphatically. "Your inside is showing for a change. You look as beautiful outside as you are inside."

Emily's face got hot, as it always did when she blushed. She'd been so combative with her sister for so long it was still hard for her to believe that the walls between them had finally come down. *The walls I put there,* she thought.

"Thank you, Ayanna. I just thought it was time for a change." She sat on the bed, across from Ayanna.

"Well, you look just wonderful. Everyone said so."

Emily made a face as she smoothed moisturizer on her face and neck. "Not everyone. I think Todd was quite explicit in expressing his opinion," she said grouchily.

Ayanna held out her hand for the small jar of

cream and used a little on her face. "Men are truly an underdeveloped species when it comes to expressing themselves properly. Don't pay him any mind, honey. He was knocked out by your new look and lost the connection between his brain and his big mouth."

Emily shrugged her shoulders. "It doesn't really matter what he thinks of my appearance. He already told me that he'd made a huge mistake in getting with me, so I'm not surprised that he thought I looked bad."

"What do you mean, getting with you?" Ayanna's eyes narrowed, and she looked ready to fight for her younger sister.

"Crap. I didn't mean to tell you this, but here's the short version." Emily sighed and launched into a terse narrative of the days she'd spent with Todd on Hilton Head. "And then he said he'd made a mistake and he left there like the hounds of hell were after him."

Ayanna's face had changed expressions several times while Emily was talking. She looked both angry and puzzled. "Are you serious? He just left and you never heard from him again?"

"Not exactly," Emily said. "He called me a few times and he sent me a bunch of plants, but I know a consolation prize when I see one, and I'd heard enough of his miserable excuses, so I didn't answer his calls. I prefer a clean break."

"Plants and phone calls, hmm?" Ayanna was tapping her chin with one finger.

"Yes, and emails, which I also ignored."

"Emmie, hon, I think there's been a huge miscommunication going on here. I think Todd has some real feelings for you and you haven't let him express them."

"I think he expressed himself quite nicely tonight. 'What have you done to yourself'—that's pretty darned expressive if you ask me."

"I didn't say he was good at speaking from his heart. Most men suck at it. But look, he went out to the airport to pick you up," she pointed out.

"Oh yeah, he was more than happy to tell me that. He said he saw me talking to a guy and he had no idea it was me. Real flattering," Emily sneered.

"What guy? Is he nice?" Ayanna was immediately curious.

"Very nice guy," Emily said confidently. "I met him on the plane. He lives in Chicago but he's moving to Columbia to open a new restaurant. His name is Jared Van Buren and I'm having lunch with him tomorrow."

"Where? At Van Buren's or 515?"

"At Van Buren's. Have you eaten there? How's the food?" Emily wanted to know.

"We've eaten at both of his restaurants and everything is fantastic. I mean ultra, ultra good.

Yum. And he's quite a dish, too. He's a very hot commodity these days. He's tall, handsome and rich, and he's straight and he can cook. He's even compassionate. He has some kind of program where he feeds people who are in need of a meal. And you met him on a plane. Go figure." Ayanna gave her sister a wicked grin and a little fist bump. "Women all over Chicago are trying to meet him and you stumble over him on a freakin' plane. I love it." She thought for a moment and laughed.

"That's why Todd had his boxers in a bunch. He saw you with that good-looking hunk and he got jealous! That's why he was being a jerk," she informed Emily.

"And he did a bang-up job. First-rate," she added with a big yawn.

Ayanna yawned back, and they agreed it was time for sleep. But Ayanna, like older sisters the world over, had to have the last word. "Don't be too hard on Todd, Emmie. He's a good man. He really is. You remember when Alex was sick with MRSA and how good he was to us through that whole ordeal. He's a wonderful guy. Give him a chance and you'll see."

Emily rolled her eyes at her sister's back as she left the room. *Yeah, I'll see how it feels for him to make a fool out of me again. No thanks, I'll pass,* she thought as she gave her pillows an extra hard punch before turning out the table lamp.

* * *

The sky was blue, the sun was shining and the temperature was cold and crisp. Emily, despite having a long, tortuous night of erotic dreams about the wonderful good guy Todd, at least looked as if she was well rested even though she wasn't. An energetic run through the neighborhood and a nice hot shower could put a glow on anybody's skin, even if that person was nursing a grudge. And she was mature enough to acknowledge that she was still harboring a big ol' chunk of resentment. She wasn't quite sure what she'd been expecting when she encountered Todd with her new hair, new clothes and new attitude, but his hostile appraisal had stung. The plan was for him to see her, realize what a fool he'd been and spend the rest of his life regretting his stupidity. He wasn't supposed to look at her with scorn and then have the big brass *cojones* to kiss her and then walk out on her. As far as her responding to his kiss and dreaming about him all night, well, that just made the whole episode a giant "fail."

But she did have some consolations, she mused as she finished putting on her makeup. She'd met Jared, who was great-looking, personable and who was treating her to lunch at his restaurant. That would be fun; Emily liked eating at new places. Her mother and sister were proud of her, and she felt closer to them than ever, which was great. And it was almost her birthday, too. Lucie and Ayanna had cooked up some kind of celebration for her, and even though they weren't giving out details, she knew it would be fun. So there was no reason at all for her to be concerned about Dr. Todd Wainwright.

She went downstairs in full battle dress; charcoal-gray wide-legged, wool trousers, ankle boots with three-inch heels, a cream-colored cashmere sweater with a wide belt to show off her waist and big silver hoop earrings with a wide silver cuff bracelet. She picked up a very thin wool stole with a woven pattern in camel and gray and went downstairs to get her coat, as well as a final inspection. Sure enough, Lucie and Ayanna stopped whatever they'd been doing in the kitchen to come see her off.

"Perfect! Your friend Jared is going to be dazzled," Lucie said.

"Thanks, Mom. Ayanna, are you sure about me taking your car? I can take a cab," Emily offered again.

"Girl, please. Don't even worry about it. It has GPS, so you can't get lost. Have a good time and bring us some dessert." Ayanna grinned.

"Of course I will," Emily said. "I'll be back in a couple of hours."

"Take your time, sweetie. If you do get lost, you can call Todd. That restaurant isn't too far from where he lives. And his hospital is near there, too," Lucie said innocently.

Emily folded the shawl in half and made a chic loop around her neck the way Sherri had showed her. "I'm sure I won't get lost, Mom. And if I do, I'll call Jared," she drawled. She took the car keys from Ayanna and laughed at the expression on Lucie's face as she left the house.

Ayanna poked her mother in the arm. "Mama, I told you to lay off the Todd thing. She's a little salty with him right now."

"I know, but I've got to look out for the poor man. I really think he's crazy about her. It's not his fault that he's a little emotionally, um, slow." They looked at each other and burst out laughing.

Todd wasn't a happy man. He was still smarting over his idiocy from the night before, and he hadn't decided how to achieve a return to Emily's good graces. Plus, he was horny as hell. Any normal man would be in the same condition if he'd had to suffer through the sizzling dreams Todd had endured all night. From a scientific viewpoint he knew that the most vivid parts of his dreams had lasted only a few minutes, but those minutes were imprinted on his brain and wreaking havoc with his body. He'd had the cold shower, he'd worked out his aggressions on the treadmill and other exercise equipment, and it hadn't done a bit of good. He wasn't feeling any better about his situation.

Deciding that food might help, he went to the kitchen area of his loft. The place had been pretty generic when he bought it, but his sister-in-law, Billie, had hooked it up for him. She'd been a high-fashion model, but she'd traded the runway for a contractor's license, and her skills were exceptional. He opened his fancy rubbed-bronze refrigerator and stared at the contents. He decided to make an omelet, despite the fact that he hadn't made one since he left Hilton Head. Cooking for Emily had been very enjoyable, before he screwed everything up.

It wasn't as if he'd done it deliberately; he'd used an extremely poor choice of words to tell Emily that he shouldn't have rushed into making love with her. What he was trying to convey was that he wanted them to have a real relationship, one that wasn't fueled purely by sex, even though the sex they'd shared was hot, wild and satisfying. He'd been trying to say that he was falling in love with her and that she deserved all of him. He wanted to share more than his body with her; he wanted to share everything, getting to know her the way a man knows the woman he wants to be with forever.

"But that's not what I said," he said aloud. "What I said was 'this is a mistake.' No, a *huge* mistake, that's what *I* said. Good move, Wainwright—real smooth." Talking to himself was a habit he'd developed in med school, a habit he indulged in only when he was frustrated and stressed out. Being a trauma physician in the biggest E.R. in Chicago was more than enough stress on a daily basis; adding Emily to the mix was a little too much.

"I'm supposed to be better than that, yet I manage to put my foot in it so tough that Emily will probably hate me forever. She was already mad at me, and when I finally see her face-to-face I piss her off all over again," he said angrily as he beat the eggs so hard they almost cried out for mercy.

"Okay, so I was surprised when I saw her because she looked different. But did I have to ask her what the hell she did to herself? That was just stupid."

Emily had looked like a different woman, so much so that he hadn't recognized her at the airport. It was a shock, but it wasn't a bad one; quite the opposite, actually. He'd had an immediate physical response to her new appearance, which made him defensive, especially when he remembered seeing her at O'Hare with a strange man drooling all over her. The image of her smiling up at that jackass, whoever he was, flashed into Todd's head and made him add a few choice words of profanity to his monologue. The sound of his doorbell distracted him; who the hell was dropping in on him out of the blue?

He went to the door in his jeans and bare feet. He hadn't bothered to put on a shirt, and whoever the hell it was would have to take him as he was. He didn't really appreciate uninvited visitors. When he looked through the peephole in the big door, his mood didn't improve. It was Cecily, a pretty little airhead he'd stopped seeing months ago. He opened the door and gave her a less-than-pleasant look.

"How did you get in here without me buzzing you in? And why are you here anyway?" He was being rude and he knew it, but it probably went right over Cecily's pretty little head. That was no reason to be deliberately nasty, however. Despite her silliness, Cecily was a good person and she didn't deserve to be verbally abused.

"Hello, baby," she cooed. "I've been thinking about you and I was in the neighborhood, so I buzzed your neighbor downstairs and he let me in," she said, sounding rather proud of herself for being so clever. She slipped past him, stroking his pecs as she entered the loft.

"Why didn't you buzz me if you wanted to come up? Why are you bothering the other people in this building?" he asked testily.

"Because you wouldn't have let me in," she

replied. "I would've called but you have me blocked," she added, taking off her busy faux fur coat. Cecily's heavily made-up eyes blinked like a wind-up toy. Her look had changed; she'd gone from emulating Rihanna to being what appeared to be a Nicki Minaj clone, complete with weirdly colored contact lenses and a shiny black Cleopatra-style wig. *At least it wasn't pink,* he thought.

"Cecily, if you knew I didn't want to talk to you, don't you think that means I didn't want to see you, either?"

"Not really. I just thought you were busy," she said coyly as she tossed her head in what she thought was a sexy gesture. It made Todd think she was going to give herself whiplash if she didn't cut it out.

She had walked over to the counter that separated the kitchen area from the living room, moving in an exaggeratedly seductive manner so he couldn't miss her new behind in her very short, very tight white sweater dress and white leather thigh-high boots. She'd either had implants or she was wearing booty pads. Cecily had a nice figure, but nice apparently wasn't good enough for her. *God, for her sake I hope those are pads.*

He left the room long enough to put on a shirt before she got any ideas. When he came back he went back to the counter and dumped out the eggs and started cleaning up the mess he'd made. He'd lost his taste for an omelet. "Cecily, what do you want?"

She batted her expertly applied false lashes at him. "Well, how about a glass of wine?"

"It's barely noon and you're talking about alcohol? You can have some water," he said tersely. "Now how about you stop playing games and tell me what you want. We stopped seeing each other once you met that NBA player, remember? What happened to all that love you were in?"

He felt a little guilty about bringing that up because he was making it sound as if he'd been affected by the breakup, which wasn't even close to the truth. He was about to end things with her when she took up with a basketball player and told him they were through. It had been one of the best days of Todd's dating life, but he saw no reason to throw it in her face. His appetite gone, he rinsed the bowl and utensils and put them in the dishwasher as he talked.

Cecily began playing with her perfectly manicured nails and avoided making direct eye contact with him. "It didn't work out. He was just taking a break before he married his baby mama," she said disdainfully. "He was treating me real nice at first, then he started acting like I was kind of a groupie, just because I'm a video model. I make good money doing what I do and I'm not a whore, so I don't know where he gets off treating me any ol' way."

Todd stifled a groan. This scenario was way high on his list of things to avoid at all costs: comforting a former lover when her new love affair went sour. He didn't want to offer her a shoulder to cry on, and offering her commonsense advice was sure to backfire. He just wanted to get rid of her as quickly as possible. "Sorry it didn't work out. Look, I need to get something to eat before I go to work, so I was just about to leave."

"Oh. Okay," she sighed. "I wouldn't want to hold you up. Maybe we can get together later," she said with a tiny glimmer of hope in her eyes.

Todd was already putting on his shoes and shoving his wallet in his jeans. He didn't have it in him to offer up the universal lame line "I'll call you," because he had no intention of doing so. He'd already parted ways with her once, and there was no reason to give her any encouragement. Personally, he thought she needed to take some time off from dating and work on her self-esteem, but he was sure she wouldn't listen to him if he suggested it. He retrieved her flashy faux fur coat from the sofa, where she'd dropped it, and held it out so she could put it on. "Cecily, I think you'd agree that we don't have a lot in common. It wouldn't be a good idea for us to try to have a relationship," he said gently but firmly.

She slipped into the coat and turned to face him with a seductive smile that looked cheap and inappropriate. "I just want to have fun, baby. Who wants a relationship?"

"I do," Todd said. He was just as surprised as she was to hear the words, but he wasn't taking them back.

He looked at her closely as they went down in the elevator. Cecily had some good qualities, although she had some unfortunate gold-digging tendencies and a dicey choice of career. She couldn't shake her plastic booty forever; what did she plan to do when her dancing days were over? He broke his own rule and said something like that to her, suggesting that she think about going to college and embarking on a real career. As he feared, her eyes filled with tears, and he didn't have a tissue or handkerchief to offer her. She did have some tissues and she was blotting her eyes as they left the elevator.

"Look, Cecily, I didn't mean to hurt your feelings. I'm really concerned about you," he said.

"I know you are and I really appreciate it. You're the only person who's tried to keep it real with me in a long time," she confessed. "And you're probably right. I need to try to do something other than dance around half-naked behind those little no-talent boys." Her voice was low and composed, and she sounded so mature it shocked Todd. She looked up at him with a serious face and said, "I've been thinking about going back to Omaha for a while now. I started out to be a nurse, believe it or not. I want to finish my degree."

Todd raised his eyebrows in surprise. "Good for you, Cecily. I'm glad you're thinking about a plan for your life. I wish you the best," he said sincerely.

They exited the building and she impulsively threw her arms around him and planted a big kiss right on his mouth. Todd could have done without the sticky synthetic goop on her mouth, but it was a nice moment and a good ending. If he'd known that he was being observed, he wouldn't have thought so.

Chapter 13

Emily found her way to Jared's restaurant with very little effort, thanks to his good directions and the GPS system in Ayanna's car. She parked in the employee lot, as Jared had told her to, and as soon as she got out of the car, Jared was standing there to escort her inside. He smiled down at her and admitted that he'd been waiting for her.

"I had one of the busboys keeping an eye out for you."

"Well, that was nice of you, Jared." She tried not to stare at him, but she had to look him over. He really was as handsome as she remembered. Nice manners, too; he held the door open and took her coat, handing it to the hostess before he showed her their table. It was a far booth that was rather private, but it offered a nice view of the place so she could take it all in.

"This is my favorite table. I can see everything but it's hard to see me. This way my team can't find me," he said with a laugh.

"Smart," Emily said with a grin. "I like this place, Jared. It's stylish but not pretentious." The main dining room had high ceilings, hardwood floors, glass subway tiles on the walls and slate tabletops. The clever lighting gave it the intimacy and elegance of a well-established steak house, but it was totally contemporary in appearance. Lunch was delicious and Jared was very good company. They had a great conversation, and she'd left the place feeling as if she'd gained a new friend.

She was sure she'd remember the way back to Ayanna's house without the GPS, but she got a little lost in the neighborhood around Van Buren's. While she tried to get the GPS to cooperate, she made a wrong turn, and in doing so she wandered down Washington. She glanced up at a big building just long enough to see a woman doing what was obviously a walk of shame with a tall, handsome man. She might have believed it was just two friends walking down the street, but the two of them went into a passionate clutch right there on the sidewalk, and Emily immediately recognized the man as Todd. Nice. And this is what passed for a good man in Ayanna's world? Emily clenched her teeth together so tightly that she was endangering years of expensive dental work, but she was too angry to notice. *Good man, my ass; he's a jerk. A whorish jerk at that.*

Her face was hot with anger when she finally saw the right street, which made her sigh with relief. She was even madder than she'd been last night, even though she wasn't ready to admit why she was so angry. She had no ties on Todd and he certainly didn't have any on her, but that didn't excuse his actions, as far as she was concerned. Instead of admiring her when he saw her new look, he'd gotten all self-righteous and preachy. Then he'd had the nerve to put his hands all over her as though she was easy. She had a little bit of trouble with that one, because she had participated in the lusty kiss and enjoyed it, too. But the irrational little voice in her head reminded her that he'd acted as if she was some borderline hoochie, when apparently hoochies were what he craved.

Her hands tightened on the steering wheel and she could feel her anger mounting, mixed with hurt feelings that she couldn't understand. Maybe it was because she'd fantasized about their encounter a little bit too much. She'd been logical and grounded all of her adult life, never allowing herself to indulge in hot, sultry daydreams about hot, sexy men. Then she lost all control with Todd in those passion-filled days on Hilton Head, until he'd told her it was all a mistake. Emily's eyes actually got teary when she remembered the pain that had cut through her at those words. She had put on a brave and stoic face, but if she was going to be honest with herself, she had to admit that he'd broken her heart.

When they were on Hilton Head, she had just come to the realization that she'd fallen in love with him. And what seemed like a minute later he told her that he didn't want her. She had been his intellectual equal but she wasn't hot enough for him, and she knew it. What pained her most were the stupid flowers and phone calls after he left. As if he was trying to soften the blow with some cheap consolation prizes or something, while trying to make himself feel better. She might have been inexperienced, but she didn't fall for that crap.

She should have just buried herself in a new project at work; that would have gotten her out of her funk. But instead she'd poured her heart out to her BFFs and she'd let them persuade her that with a few little changes she'd look so good that any man would find her irresistible. It had worked with Jared; he'd found her very attractive. But Todd hadn't. Not only could he resist her, he could even hook up with another woman the day after he saw her in her newfound glory. Emily muttered several curse words under her breath and pounded the steering wheel. Why couldn't he have fallen madly in love with her at first sight, the way he was supposed to? She ripped her glove off with her teeth and used the back of her hand to dash away the tears that kept trying to fall. She sure didn't want her mother and her sister to see her all weak and weepy.

She wasn't used to feeling either helpless or hopeless, yet he'd made her feel both ways. And she truly resented Todd for that. Or maybe she was mad at herself for allowing him to affect her so deeply. She turned on to the street where Ayanna lived and set her jaw firmly. She had too much sense to let that joker get the upper hand with her. The evil little voice in her head kept needling at her and finally planted a twisted idea in her brain. This was the ultimate revenge; before she left Chicago, she was going to fix him once and for all. There was nothing like payback to put a man like him in his place, and she knew just the way to do it.

She was going to seduce him, screw his brains out and dump him, all before she went back to her life in Columbia and lived happily ever after. It was an evil, devious way to get him but good, and she was going to enjoy every single second of it.

* * *

Emily wasn't sure how soon she could get started on her plan to get back at Todd, but she was eager to get going. So when she found out that he'd be joining them for dinner, she was thrilled. Lucie had barely asked her how her lunch with Jared was before she announced that Billie had invited them over to dinner that night.

"That was nice of her," Emily said as she hung up her coat in the hall closet. "What's the occasion?"

"It's just that they like to rotate the entertaining during the holidays," Lucie said innocently. "That way no one's overwhelmed with too much cooking. And her parents are visiting for the holidays, so they want to have everyone over." She waited a moment before delivering the best part. "And Todd is off today, so he'll be able to come, too. Won't that be nice?"

Emily hid her sly smile of triumph before turning away from the closet. "You bet. It'll be really nice to see him again. Now, where are my beautiful nieces? When do Alex and Cameron get home from school?" She kept up a steady stream of chatter as she and Lucie went up to the girls' bedroom to see if they were awake and ready to play. Her Blackberry rang while she was walking and when she saw Todd's name on the caller ID, she smirked in triumph.

"Hello?" She sounded airy and carefree, as if she was actually glad to hear his voice.

"Hello, Emily. I told you I was going to call today. How are you doing?"

She rolled her eyes at his lack of panache. "Just fine, thanks, and you?"

They had a brief conversation and she was as pleasant as possible, even a bit flirtatious. She wanted him to be completely off his guard when she put her plan into action. There was no reason for him to suspect that she was going to bring him down and enjoy doing it. Step one of the plan was in motion; now she had to find something classy and sexy to wear for the evening.

Todd was getting dressed to go to his brother's house when he realized that he was nervous at the prospect of seeing Emily. It was taking him like five times longer to get ready than it normally did, for one thing. His usual routine was to take a quick shower and throw on whatever was clean. It should have taken him less time than that because he'd already had a shower that day. Feeling that he wanted to have a fresh start with Emily and make the best impression possible, he took the time to lay his clothes out on the bed before taking his second shower of the day. He'd put his foot in it a couple of times already. Last night had been the zenith of his stupid behavior, and he was determined to look and act his best tonight. This might be the last chance he had to get into her good graces, and he couldn't blow it.

When he arrived at Billie and Jason's he was sartorially splendid in an expensive pair of wool slacks and a cashmere pullover that had been a gift from Billie the previous Christmas. Jason opened the door and gave him a diabolical grin as he looked him up and down.

"Don't you look cute in your nice coat," he drawled. "And you brought wine, too. If I didn't know you I'd think you were a perfect gentleman."

Todd was in no mood for his older brother's jokes. "Screw you," he muttered. "Where's Billie?"

He took off his overcoat and tossed it at Jason as he went in search of his gorgeous sister-in-law, finding her in the kitchen. Kissing her on the cheek, he asked what he could do to help her.

"Not much, sweetie. You could toss the green salad if you want to. Everything else is done." Her eyes widened as she looked at the two bottles of wine he'd selected. "Wow, this is really nice. Thanks, Todd."

"I thought you might like it," he said with a smile. He washed his hands and went right to work on the salad. When Jason entered the room, he looked even more amused by his brother.

"I've never seen you so domestic before," he said. "You must be trying to impress somebody."

Jason's in-laws joined in the conversation, which was a relief to Todd. Lee Phillips was a lovely, calm woman he admired. "You look very handsome, Todd, but you always do," she said, tilting her face for his customary kiss on the cheek.

Her husband, Boyd, was more inclined to razz Todd, just as Jason had. "Who could you be trying to impress? Since we're all old married folks, it must be Ayanna's little sister," he said drolly. "You need some tips on how to impress a lady? Because Jason and I can probably help a brother out in that regard. All you have to do is ask."

"I'm good, Boyd. I think I can handle this," Todd said with a smile.

Billie handed the wine to Jason. "I'm going upstairs for a minute. Don't pick on your brother. And Daddy, don't you pick on Todd, either. In fact, why don't you get the door. That's probably Nick and Dakota." She went upstairs, her father and mother went to the door and Jason continued his lighthearted harassment.

"I know I'm getting all in your business but I can't help it, man. You gave me a real hard time when I fell for Billie, as I recall, so I have to return the favor. It looks to me like you're trying to get on Emily's good side tonight, am I right?"

"Yeah, so what if I am?" Todd looked up from the salad with a frown.

"I'm just giving you a hard time, bro. Much like

you did when I was making a fool out of myself over Billie," he reminded him. "You look good, almost as good as me. So why don't you leave that to me and go handle coats or something. Emily and the rest of them should be here any minute. Relax, man, this is going to be a good night."

Todd was willing to concede that Jason had been right; it was a great evening. The food, the music, the conversation and the atmosphere were all perfect, but Todd barely noticed. He was too taken with Emily to pay much attention to anything else that was going on. She seemed warm and friendly, instead of being aloof and cold, which was what he deserved and expected from her. He managed to sit across from her at dinner and even though the food was delicious, he would have had a hard time describing the meal to anyone. She looked absolutely beautiful, every part of her. It was the first time that he'd looked at her objectively since she'd cut her hair. He'd been so full of himself last night that all he'd registered about her appearance was the fact that she didn't look the way he remembered her. The unadorned face and the comfortable clothes had been replaced, along with her natural hair, but what had replaced those things was just as wonderful, now that he took the time to really look.

Her hair was smooth, but it didn't look artificial

and overdone. She was wearing makeup, but not very much. Even he could see that it was just enough to bring out her features instead of covering her like a mask. Her clothes were certainly different from the things she'd worn on Hilton Head, but they were tasteful and fit her well. He could finally see that she was the same woman, just gently enhanced. This was the same Emily he'd fallen for. And he'd messed that budding relationship up totally. But he was going to put it back together if it was the last thing he ever did.

The custom was for the men to do the cleaning up, since the women usually did most of the cooking, and tonight was no exception. The ladies were relaxing in the great room, laughing and talking over the dessert the men had served, while the men put away leftovers and loaded the dishwasher. Todd was doing his part to assist, although it was plain from his expression that his mind wasn't on his task. He was totally concentrated on getting back to Emily's good side. When she came into the kitchen with a stack of dessert plates and a handful of forks, her arrival made Todd's face light up.

"Hi, guys! I thought I'd be useful and save you a trip," she said cheerfully. Todd took the things from her hands at once, chiding her gently.

"You should have just left these for us. This is just how we do things here. We wait on you," he reminded her.

Jason stepped in and surprised Todd to no end by being helpful for once. "Todd, why don't you take Emily out and show her the Christmas lights," he suggested. "Take her down Lakeshore Drive and show her the sights."

Todd could only hope that his overwhelming gratitude didn't make him look like a total fool. Trying for casually debonair, he turned to Emily and asked if she'd like to go.

"Absolutely," she said with a big smile. "Let me tell Ayanna and Mom that I'm leaving and I'll get my coat."

"No, *I'll* get your coat," Todd said, following her as she left the room.

Chapter 14

It seemed like a corny idea, to go riding around to look at Christmas lights, but it was the perfect opening Emily had been waiting for. She was a bit relieved to leave the house, truth be told. She felt just a little out of place among all the happy, gorgeous married people. Ayanna and Johnny, Billie and Johnny, Nick and Dakota, plus their gorgeous children; it was just a bit much for her. She didn't have anything in her life to match their domestic bliss; all she had was an abnormal bunch of diplomas and awards and certifications, most of which weren't even framed. In addition, she also felt the beginnings of a giant crisis of conscience.

These were truly decent people who'd managed to find love and were lucky enough to start beautiful families. And here she was, skulking around trying to start some mess. The twinkle of the beautiful Christmas lights down Lakeshore Drive felt like little pricks in her heart or something. Guilt began to nibble at her toes and work its way up her body. But Todd's cell phone rang, and it wasn't the same ringtone she remembered from yesterday. It was a musical version of the universally recognized tune from many, many porn movies, the "boom-chicka-wow-wow" sound. And he answered it quickly, instead of ignoring it.

The woman on the other end was speaking loud enough to wake the dead, so Emily could hear every word. She wanted Todd to come to her place for a late dinner or early breakfast or Roman orgy or something. Emily stared fixedly out the window and deliberately ignored the conversation. The guilt vanished, leaving steely resolve in its place. Any man who had a separate "hot hoochie" ringtone for his adoring fans and who juggled women with no shame was ripe to get taken down. She was actually grateful the call had come in. While she waited for him to get off the phone, she looked around the SUV.

The interior of Todd's vehicle was like an intimate cocoon just for the two of them. His iPod provided low, sexy music, and the climate control made it warm and comfortable. Outside, the sparkling lights really were enchanting to observe. Emily willed herself to be relaxed. Although she was pretty angry, she wasn't practiced in deceit. She wanted to start a casual conversation that sounded genuine, but she didn't trust herself to do it well. Todd, however, showed no reticence at all. As soon as the call was over, he opened right up.

"This was the best idea Jason's ever had, other than marrying Billie. I've been thinking about you all day," he said charmingly. "All night long I've been trying to think of a way to get you alone, and this was the perfect opportunity." He reached over to take her hand, and she was so startled she had to fight the urge to jump.

"This is nice," she agreed. "But why did you need to get me alone? That sounds kind of ominous."

"On the contrary, I owe you an apology. Many, many apologies, as a matter of fact. And I've missed you, Emily. I had one of the best times of my life with you and I screwed it up with my big mouth."

She stared at him, glad that the interior darkness made it impossible for him to see the look of disdain on her face. How the hell did men do that? Todd sounded so damned sincere, as if he meant every word he was saying. The guy was good, she'd give him that. "So you missed me and you owe me an apology," she murmured. "Is that your story?"

"That would be the condensed version of my story. The long version is that I've said things I didn't mean and I handled things badly and I find you irresistible and I want to get to know you all over again." He clasped her hand, giving it a firm, gentle pressure.

Emily hesitated only a second before putting her free hand on top of his and stroking it, using the sensitive tips of her fingers to trace gentle patterns on his warm skin.

"That sounds like an interesting basis for discussion, at the very least. When do you suggest we get started?" she asked in a voice that she hoped was just low and sexy enough to entice him without sounding ridiculous.

The sound of his voice when he replied "How about right now" let her know that she had succeeded. *So let the game begin.*

"Todd, this place is gorgeous. Did you decorate this yourself?" Emily was looking around his spacious loft with great interest and admiration. After Todd made his "getting to know you better" play, it had taken them a surprisingly short time to get to his building. He put away their coats and turned on the music before going to the kitchen area to pour something to drink while Emily explored the place. She was completely sincere in her compliment; the place was a triumph of modern design.

It had high ceilings, heated hardwood floors, exterior walls that were the original brick and oxidized copper tiles on the interior walls. Huge windows gave him a great view of the city, and there were even more features and amenities that she'd never seen before.

"I didn't do anything but write checks," Todd admitted. "My sister-in-law, Billie, did all of this. She used to be a model, but now she renovates houses. And I mean she does the contracting work, not just design. Look at these glass tiles in the kitchen. She put them up herself," he said proudly.

Emily walked over to take a look. The kitchen was stupendous, and the green glass subway tiles were beautiful. There was a glass counter at the bar that was about an inch thick and travertine marble on the floor. "I've never seen anything like this," Emily murmured. "I can tell you from experience that tile is pretty tricky to put up correctly, especially glass tile. I am really impressed. Can I see the rest of it?"

Todd took her hand and led her around through the rest of the place, consisting of a huge bedroom area, an office space and the bathroom, which looked like a photo in an upscale design magazine. The dwelling was open and airy, yet designed for privacy with opaque glass pocket doors to separate the bed and bath from visitors. Todd seemed pleased with her enjoyment of his home as he led her back to the living room. He seated her on one of his long leather sofas and picked up a remote control.

"Okay, this is like one of my favorite parts of the place. Watch this," he said. He pointed the remote at a slate table with a large aquarium on it. It was half-filled with glass pebbles and there was no water and no fish. Suddenly a fire began to flicker, to her surprise. He pointed it at a copper wall sculpture and water began trickling down.

"Now that's just brilliant," Emily said. "Billie can build a house for me any time."

Todd was next to her on the sofa by then, using the handy remote to lower all the other lights in the room. "She's a great contractor and designer and mom. She's just a fantastic woman, period. She and Jason are so happy together it's ridiculous. I've never known Jason to be so content in his whole life. My brother is an extremely fortunate man to be married to her."

Emily didn't doubt his sincerity, but his words annoyed her for some reason. How hypocritical of Todd to be praising his brother's marriage when she knew what a whore he was. She sipped her drink moodily and was jarred back to the moment by his hand on hers. She turned to face him with a carefully concealed smile. He was looking at her so intently that she had to break the silence. If he wanted to say something, she'd help him out. She found it difficult to look into his eyes, for some reason, so she fixed her gaze on his lower lip.

"This is really good, Todd. What is it?"

"Some organic nonalcoholic spumante I got. Passion fruit and raspberry."

"Nonalcoholic? Really?"

"I can't be drinking if I'm going to drive you home." He ran a finger down the side of her cheek. "I couldn't let anything happen to you."

It would have been music to her ears if it had been anybody but Todd speaking the words. It was annoyingly sweet to hear him say them because they meant nothing but they sounded so true. She put her almost-empty glass on the console table behind the sofa and turned to face him. He kept talking to her in that damnably sexy voice.

"I told you that I owe you some major apologies. First of all, last night's performance was just ridiculous. I had no business going off on you like that. It was pure jealousy, that's what it was."

Emily looked bemused. "Jealous of Jared? Seriously jealous, Todd? I find that hard to believe."

He gave a harsh laugh. "Believe it, baby. I was ready to snap him in half like a twig. I'm not proud of it, but I own it," he said candidly.

"That's just one of my transgressions, as you

well know. Last night, I was very negligent in not telling you how gorgeous you are. I was so surprised when I saw you that my common sense took a vacation and instead of complimenting you, I acted like an idiot." He shook his head and looked genuinely regretful. "You have to know that I truly thought you were perfect when we were together on Hilton Head. I really did. I meant everything I said to you. You were and are a beautiful, beautiful woman. It just never occurred to me that you could improve on perfection." He put his hand into her soft hair and stroked it gently.

Staring at his mouth wasn't a good idea after all. He had a slightly pouty lower lip that she knew for a fact could work magic, so she tried actually looking into his eyes. Mistake number two. His eyes were filled with what appeared to be honest admiration and real feeling. She'd never really appreciated his eyes, but they were one of his best features. They were large and expressive and fringed with long eyelashes that a lot of women would have killed for, or at the very least, they'd pay a lot of money to attain them. He sounded as if he meant every word he was saying and he looked both sexy and romantic, but she had to ignore that if she wanted to keep the upper hand. She pounced on the last thing he'd said, something about her improving on perfection.

"If that's the case, why didn't you say so? Why

did you act like I'd turned into a cheap hoochie?" she asked tartly.

"Because I'm not that bright," he admitted. "I don't blame you for not letting me off the hook. I deserve it. Go ahead and let me have it. Yell at me, talk about me and call me names, whatever you want to do. And when the dust settles, I'll still be here because I really do want to make a new start with you."

She had tried to look away again, but his eyes were so intense she couldn't do it. "I don't know what to say."

"You don't have to say anything, Emmie. Words aren't the only way to show someone what's on your mind. We already know I don't do too well with words. I want to show you how I feel about you, because it's very important to me that you know."

"It is?"

"More important than anything," he replied.

He moved closer to her, still playing with her hair. When he bent in for a kiss, Emily didn't even think about stopping him. She just leaned in to meet him, and their mouths connected in the kind of kiss she remembered all too well. His lips and tongue played over hers, and she gave him back the same passion until they were both breathless. Emily's arms went around his neck, and he pulled her gently into his lap as they continued kissing.

When they finally came up for air, Todd was the first to speak.

"That's what I wanted to say, Emmie."

Emily looked at him intently before lowering her eyelids slightly. "Are you sure? We were a big mistake, remember? Those were your words, not mine."

"I told you I'm not that bright. Talking isn't the best thing I do, apparently. I sure messed things up with you. I was trying to say one thing and it came out all wrong." He tipped her face up with one long finger and kissed her again; outlining her lips with his tongue and tasting her as if she was a Godiva chocolate. "I hope you can believe me," he added as he ran his hands up and down her arms. He fingered her soft violet sweater. "You look so pretty in this," he added as he kissed her neck. "And you smell, um…delicious."

Her hands stroked his chest, the sensitive tips of her long fingers tracing the solid muscles she remembered so well. She stroked the faint outline of the scar on his chest. Moving her hips slowly, she could feel the proof of his arousal against her body. She was as turned on as he was. Every time his lips touched her skin, she could feel the moist heat building in all her most sensitive parts. He murmured her name, and for a few seconds she forgot that she was on a mission. She just lost herself in his arms.

His fingers toyed with the small buttons down the front of her sweater, but he wasn't too successful in undoing them. Emily braced her hands against his shoulders and leaned away from him until she was sitting up as he leaned back into the throw pillows on the back of the sofa, watching her. She moved her hips slowly and deliberately until he moaned her name again. While he devoured her with his eyes, she carefully undid each button until he could see her violet silk camisole, trimmed in black lace. When she was finished, she pulled the sweater open to expose her black lace-covered breasts. The thin barrier of silk was the only thing between the two of them.

His eyes glazed with desire, and he sat up and lowered his head to her cleavage as he slid the sweater off her body. She shivered as she felt his breath on her and he stopped, concerned.

"Are you cold?"

She shook her head. "Not at all," she murmured, but she trembled again as he lowered the straps of the camisole and her bra.

"I think you are cold. Come with me. I'll get you nice and warm."

Before she could protest, he'd carried her into the bedroom and lowered her to his huge king-size bed. It was neatly made with cool, crisp linens and a thick comforter. On top of the comforter was a big throw that looked and felt like chinchilla. In what seemed like seconds, she was on top of its furry warmth wearing nothing but her black lace panties and he was next to her wearing nothing at all. He was right; she was now bathed in the most wonderful heat she could imagine. There was another glass fireplace in the room, this one set into the wall. The room was bathed with its flickering light.

Todd lay next to her and kissed her, long and lingering. He looked gorgeous in the firelight, and she was about to tell him so when his hands covered her breasts and his thumbs stroked her nipples, which were already hard and ready for him. His mouth covered one breast and he devoured it, using his lips, his tongue and the slightest tease of his teeth to excite her. The feel of his hot, firm lips and his tongue brought her close to the edge of a climax. She had thought she remembered what his loving felt like, but this was even better than she recalled.

He straddled her body, making it easier for him to pleasure both her breasts. Their hands found each other and their fingers laced together. She was moaning and saying his name as he kissed his way down her body, licking her navel as he began to pull off her thong. She raised her hips off the bed to help him and just when he began to achieve their mutual goal, his phone rang. Emily froze, wondering what he was going to do. To her horror, he answered it on the first ring.

"Dr. Wainwright. Yes, okay. How many? Okay, I'll be there in twenty minutes. You know what I need. See you soon."

His voice and demeanor had changed completely. He was off the bed and the firelight was lost as he turned on the bedside lamp. Emily took the ends of the furry throw and covered her body. "What's going on, Todd?"

He leaned over and kissed her mouth gently but quickly. "I'm on call tonight. I traded with another doctor so I could have the next two nights off," he said as he was hastily pulling on clean underwear. "I wanted to make sure I could be with you on your birthday, if you wanted me there." His voice trailed off as he went into the closet for jeans and a thick tweed sweater. He pulled socks out of a drawer and sat down to put them on.

"You do want me there, right? I'm not imagining things, am I?" He looked at her over his shoulder as he put on the second sock.

Emily smiled; she couldn't seem to help it. "No, you're not imagining things. Can I get a cab to get back to Ayanna's?"

Todd was in constant motion, even as he was talking. He got a navy blue velour robe out of the closet and handed it to her. "Sweetheart, it's too far. If you don't mind waiting here, I'll take you home as soon as I'm done. I'm only five minutes from the hospital and it may not be as bad as they think," he mumbled as he went out of the room.

Emily put the robe on and followed him. He was already in his boots and was putting on his coat. "Listen, baby, is this okay, I mean staying here? I hate to put you out, but I can't plan for emergencies."

"It's fine. Don't worry about it. I'll be here when you get back."

He gave her the wide, joyful smile that had always attracted her. He held her tight for a long hug and one last kiss. "There are remotes for everything and there's food in the refrigerator if you get hungry. I'll be back as soon as I can."

And with that the door closed behind him. It was so strange to see him in action. He was a trauma surgeon at a very busy urban hospital and he was bound to get called in on emergencies. Somehow Emily had stopped thinking about the sum total of the man. She had been too busy concentrating on the part of him that had hurt her so badly. This was something she hadn't expected at all. She went to find her purse and get her cell phone. She had to call Ayanna and let her know she wouldn't be back until the next day. And she had some thinking to do until then.

Chapter 15

Emily came awake slowly. Todd's bed was the best one she'd ever slept in. She was warm, well rested and so relaxed it was as if she was floating. And she was naked. It hadn't made sense for her to get dressed again, and she felt so wonderful without clothes on she just didn't put them back on. She began her usual morning stretch and quickly realized that she was floating, or at least resting, on Todd. His arms were around her, and he seemed just as comfortable as she. Obviously, he'd come back and gotten in bed with her without waking her. She was torn between being embarrassed and being aroused. On the one hand, this wasn't the way she'd imagined waking up, but on the other, she couldn't think of a better way to start the day. Her cheeks turned hot at her boldness, and she began to move away from his warmth. His arms tightened around her.

"Don't leave," he said in a voice made even deeper by sleep. "You feel so good."

His hands were stroking her bare body, caressing her butt and the sensitive spot at the base of her spine. She sighed, a sound of contentment and longing as she melted against him. Her face was cradled on his shoulder and he kissed her forehead.

"What time did you get home? What time is it now?" she murmured.

"It's about eight. I got home a couple of hours ago. Damn, you feel good. Happy birthday, sweetheart."

"It is my birthday," she said dreamily. "I forgot all about it."

"I could never forget something that important," he said.

"You have a very sexy voice, Todd."

"Don't tell me things like that. I'll start singing to you."

She giggled as she began her own exploration of his body, loving the feel of his smooth skin. Her hand went down his chest, down past his navel to seek out his manhood. It felt heavy, hard and familiar in her hand. She squeezed gently and began to explore every inch of it as he groaned in pleasure. He gently rolled her over onto her back to start an investigation of his own, starting with her lips then her neck, her shoulders and her chest, while his hand found the moist warmth between her legs. When her hips began to move, his lips followed his hand so he could explore every bit of her with his mouth. His tongue reached the center of her, licking and sucking until she reached her first climax, but he wouldn't stop until she had come again and was crying his name.

He showed her no mercy but much more passion. Every time she thought she couldn't experience more sensation, he showed her how much more he could give. He finally relented and slowly kissed his way back up her body until he was holding her close and kissing her face.

"Um, Todd, that was…" Emily pushed her hair out of her face and sighed as he continued to kiss her face with one hand cupped around her cheek.

"Yes, it was," he said. "I totally agree."

"Now it's your turn," she told him.

"That *was* my turn, baby," he said with a rakish smile.

She had to laugh at his smug expression. She held his face for a long kiss and replied, "Well then, this is my turn. Lay back, sugar."

He was even more erect than before, and he felt twice as hard. When her mouth touched him she could feel his reaction, and she licked him as she would a giant ice-cream cone on the hottest day of summer. She wanted to give him the same passionate torture he'd given her, taking him to the highest level of satisfaction possible, and he gave her every indication that she was doing just that.

"Emily, Emmie, baby, come here, damn," he moaned as he urged her to change positions so that he could enter her. Their bodies came together hard and fast. She locked her legs around his waist and he reared back so he was on his knees, thrusting his body into hers. He pumped into her sweetness until they exploded as one, finally collapsing on the bed, sweating and breathing hard.

Neither one of them said a word for a long time, but their silence spoke volumes. They stayed locked in each other's arms until they fell asleep.

"Where are you going?" Emily's eyes were half-closed and her voice was sleepy and very sexy.

Todd was getting out of bed as quietly as possible, but he'd disturbed her sleep. "I'm sorry, sweetheart. I didn't mean to wake you, but I'm needed at the hospital. I'm working a swing shift, and figured I'd go in early to check on my patients from last night." He leaned over to kiss her forehead. "I was gonna grab a quick shower and fix you breakfast."

"How about if we shower together and I fix you breakfast?"

She looked so sweet with her tangled hair and her now makeupless face that Todd felt a deep twinge in his heart. He could get used to this very quickly. "Shower it is. I think you're gonna like it."

He held his hands out to her and pulled her out of the bed, holding her close before walking her backward into the bathroom.

"This is one swanky bathroom, Todd. I did take advantage of the facilities a couple of times, and I was very impressed."

"Yeah, Billie outdid herself on this place," Todd said proudly.

The bathroom was a place of beauty. Blue-green glass tiles on the walls, heated slate tiles on the floor, custom glass counters, dual marble vessel sinks and a marble soaking tub made it look chic and modern, but the shower took it over the top. It was a stand-alone unit enclosed in glass with an elaborate panel of controls on opposing sides of the enclosure. The floor of the shower was teak, to match the cleverly designed storage units.

"I don't suppose there's an extra toothbrush to be had," Emily inquired.

Todd gave her an odd look. "Absolutely. Just don't tell Jason about this," he warned. He opened one of the cupboards and took out a case of new toothbrushes. "Help yourself. Yeah, I have dental OCD. I can't use a toothbrush more than once. Jason used to give me the business over it, and I let him think I'd outgrown what he thinks is bizarre behavior. But I didn't, so here you go. You can have a brush for every tooth if you want."

Emily dissolved in laughter when he finished his explanation. Todd pretended to be offended.

"Go ahead, laugh it up. You think I'm a lunatic, right?"

"No, I think you're adorable. Toothpaste?"

As he handed her the tube, he was struck again by how comfortable and easy this was. He'd never met a woman he wanted to be with in the morning. That was one of the reasons he'd never had one stay at the loft. And he'd never known a woman as unselfconscious and natural as Emily. Even brushing her teeth she looked as sexy as the top runway model of the moment, whoever that might be.

"Todd, this thing is way complicated." Emily was examining the panels in the shower. "You wouldn't happen to have a remote for this, would you?"

He did indeed, and he began to show her the various settings. Emily shook her head. "Just turn it on. You can show me the rest later. The heated floors are wonderful, but I'm getting cold and I don't want to make you late for work."

Todd laughed at the expression on her face when the water came on. The multiple heads with their various settings turned the shower into something like an aquatic sex toy. The water jets vibrated and pulsed and stimulated body parts in a way that had to be experienced to be believed. They tried to be quick and chaste in deference to Todd's schedule, but it was difficult.

"If you let me, I promise to make this up to you tonight. I give you my word."

Their wet, soapy arms were locked around each other's bodies while Emily's hips moved against his groin.

"I couldn't say no to that, could I?"

By mutual agreement they rinsed off. Emily was looking around for towels, but there didn't seem to be any. Todd gave her a secretive smile. "One more thing we have to thank Billie for," he said.

He stood her in front of a sleek freestanding panel with a vertical row of round vents and pushed a button. Warm air began blowing over her body, giving her yet another new sensation.

"An energy-efficient body dryer," he explained.

Her eyes closed in bliss as she experienced the ultimate finish to a perfect shower. "You're just full of surprises, Todd."

"You have no idea. Wait until tonight."

He covered her mouth with his to prevent her from asking any questions, but she didn't mind at all.

"Are you sure you want to do this?"

"Emily, I told you I have plenty of time to take you to Ayanna's house before I go to the hospital. And, yes, I'm coming in to say hello to your mother and your sister. We're two grown and sexy adults, and we have no reason to be embarrassed about anything we did from the time we left them until now. This ain't no 'walk of shame,' sweetheart. I don't know where you ladies get your crazy ideas from."

She opened her mouth to snap, "They aren't crazy notions. They are proven tenets derived from sordid dealings with trifling men," but the words wouldn't come out. It was exactly what she'd have said a few months ago, but now it would have felt as if she was uttering a foreign language. In addition, they had reached Ayanna's big brick house and there was no turning back.

Todd opened her door and gallantly helped her out of the car as though he'd been doing it forever. That, too, would have earned a snarky remark from her in the past, but she'd found that she liked it. He had nice manners and he didn't make a big show out of it, so there was no reason to be a quasifeminist bitch about it. She tightened her fingers around Todd's and prepared for the inquisition to come.

Lucie opened the door before Emily could use her key. "There you are! Happy birthday, darling," she said brightly, planting a kiss on Emily's cheek. "I made breakfast. Do you have time for a bite, Todd?" She turned her cheek to accept his kiss.

Emily raised both her eyebrows and looked over her mother's shoulder to Ayanna, who was sitting at the kitchen table drinking tea. She had a smile on her face that meant she was going to grill Emily at length at her earliest opportunity, but all she said was "Good morning, you two. And happy birthday, Em."

It was by far the strangest birthday she could remember, and it wasn't even noon. Todd gladly accepted her mother's invitation to join them. He smiled, remembering Emily and him had gotten carried away in the shower, totally forgetting their own plans for breakfast. He devoured two waffles, scrambled eggs, bacon, orange juice and coffee while making pleasant conversation as if there was nothing unusual about him bringing her home after they spent the night together.

"Thanks so much, Mrs. Porter, for the delicious meal. I truly hate to eat and run, but I do have to check in with my patients," Todd said.

"Honey, call me Lucie. And you're more than welcome. Are you taking Emmie out tonight? We always celebrate her birthday on Thanksgiving weekend since the two days are so close, but I think it would be nice to do something on her day," she said with the bright smile no male could resist.

Emily's face grew warm with chagrin. There were worse things than the legendary walk of shame. She looked to Ayanna for support, but she was laughing into her cup, the traitor.

Todd rose from the table and leaned down to kiss her, right on the mouth in front of everyone. "I happen to have something very special planned tonight. Is eight okay?"

"Yes, that's…perfect," Emily said softly.

She walked Todd to the door and watched him walk down the driveway. She braced herself for the onslaught of questions she knew she'd have to field from Lucie and Ayanna and turned around to face them. And they weren't there. She was alone in the kitchen, but she heard Lucie call to her from upstairs.

"Come on up, I want to show you something, Emmie."

She trudged up the stairs slowly, but when she got to the guest bedroom she was using, she had to laugh. Madison and Lindsey, up from their nap, were seated on her bed amidst an array of cards and presents and some shiny helium balloons.

"For me?"

"Of course, you goofy girl," Ayanna said with a laugh. "Hurry up and open them."

Lucie gave her a big hug and suggested she hurry. "You have another surprise and you don't want to be late."

Emily sat on the bed and her nieces crawled onto her lap. She felt happy and slightly dazed at the same time. This was definitely her most unusual birthday. Ever. Her mother had given her an array of Christian Dior perfume products in Miss Dior Chérie, a light, feminine scent that was just perfect. Ayanna's gift was some very sexy lingerie in a champagne color trimmed with bronze lace. It was all there, bustier, bra, thong and garter belt. She'd also given her a nice selection of hosiery. Panty hose, regular hosiery and sexily textured tights in great colors. They were just what Emily needed.

"Honey, I know the style is to go barelegged these days, but we Southern girls get too cold to go without all year-round. I pity the ones that do," Ayanna said, shaking her head.

Lucie agreed with her. "I have to have something on my legs in the winter, especially up here. I don't know how all those models and movie stars do it. I really don't."

Emily laughed. "But Mom, you're in South Carolina in the winter! It doesn't get that cold at home," she protested.

"Yes, but Columbia might not be home forever. I'm really thinking about moving to Chicago," Lucie said quietly.

Emily stared at her mother and waited for a wave of rage to cross her, but it didn't. All she felt was curiosity. "Really, Mom?"

Lucie smiled at her youngest daughter and patted her cheek. "Yes, I'm really thinking about it. I want to spend more time with my grandchildren, for one thing. And the house is much too big for me and too much to maintain by myself," she offered. "And I do love Chicago, except for the coldest parts of winter. And…"

Emily held up both hands. "Mom, you don't have to explain to me. If this would be a good change for you, go for it. I can see why you'd want a change," she said calmly.

Lucie looked relieved and Ayanna looked smug as Emily went back to trying on her new perfume and body cream. "I told you that Emily would be fine with it," Ayanna said. "Emily, hurry up and get dressed so we can go. It's time for your next surprise."

"Am I going to like it?" Emily asked and smiled.

"You're gonna love it, if we get there on time. Make haste, chick!"

Chapter 16

The next surprise was a trip to Ayanna's hair-stylist. It was a much appreciated treat because her hair was definitely looking shady after her morning of passion. The salon was a very soothing place to relax and recharge, and it also gave her a chance to talk to Ayanna.

"Thanks again for this, Ayanna. You don't have to pay for me, though."

"Don't be silly, this is part of your present. And it's a little mommy time for me. I'm devoted to my babies, but sometimes I need to remember I'm not just a mommy. So my wonderful husband is treating both of us, and Mom gets to spoil the girls rotten. So it's all good," she said cheerfully and raised her glass of sparkling mineral water.

"Now let's get down to business. At some point in the last twenty-four hours, you realized that Todd really is a wonderful guy. When and how did that happen?"

Emily shook her head and looked down at her feet, soaking in a warm whirlpool bath. "Don't say it like that, Ayanna. That makes it sound like I'm a normal, rational woman, and I'm not. I'm a very confused woman with a low moral character," she said sadly.

"What in the world are you talking about? You're not making any sense," Ayanna said worriedly.

Emily finally looked her in the eyes. "I'm not being honest with Todd. I saw him after I left Jared's restaurant yesterday. I got turned around and ended up on his street, even though I didn't know it was his street at the time. Well, there he was with this really hot chick, you know with the thigh-high boots and false eyelashes and wig." She shook her head as she remembered. "So they're kissing in the middle of the sidewalk, and it was like someone poured bleach in my eyes, or some other toxic substance. He had the nerve to criticize me for meeting a nice, decent guy on a plane, and he's in the middle of the street with the town hoochie! Plus, there was the same matter of telling me I was a mistake. I just kind of snapped, Ayanna. I decided I was going to screw him and toss him to the side before I went home. I figured he deserved it and we'd be even."

Her sister looked calm and sympathetic, instead of the hostile reaction Emily expected, since Ayanna was a big fan of Todd's. "So when did you realize that wouldn't work, honey?"

"Somewhere between the first apology and the last kiss I came back to my right mind, I guess." Her eyes filled with tears. "He was so incredibly sweet. He apologized for everything he'd done, for every time he put his foot in his mouth, for whatever. And he told me he wanted his actions to show me how he felt about me, and, oh, all kinds of things.

"Then he got called in to the hospital, and it was like seeing another side of him. And when he came back this morning, it was just… Well, you know," she ended glumly.

"So what's the problem, sis? It sounds like you've gotten everything out in the open and you're ready to take it to the next level. Why are you so upset?"

"Because *he* was honest with *me,* but I wasn't honest with him. I think he's just a much better person than I am. He was honestly trying to make things better, and I was being a vindictive cow. He deserves better than that. Than me," she clarified with a big sniff.

Ayanna patted her hand and handed her some tissue. "Emily, baby sister, please don't torture yourself like this. If you knew what I put poor Johnny through while we were dating, you'd wonder why the man ever married me. Logic and love don't always go together. When we're in love, all full of hormones and emotions and lust and longing, things are bound to go off the tracks once in a while. If you find me a couple who has never had an argument, or come close to breaking up, I'd be very surprised. People say things they don't mean and feelings get hurt, but that's just life. Not all of life, but a part of life, that's for sure."

"Yes, but…"

Ayanna shook her head. "No 'buts,' Emmie. Give yourself a break. Stop trying to convince yourself that you don't deserve to be in love and to have someone love you. Because way down deep, I think that's what this is all about. I'm older and wiser and I know these things. Let go of all the dumb stuff and enjoy yourself, not just tonight, but for always. And if I'm right, which I am, you're going to be very happy for a very long time. You'll see."

Emily was going to do her best to follow Ayanna's advice and just enjoy the moment. Todd was certainly making it very, very easy for her. When they got home from the salon, there were beautiful flowers waiting for her. They were magnificent orchids in a variety of colors that left her speechless. He was right on time to pick her up, too. She appreciated that gesture because it meant she had less time to worry. Besides that, she was ridiculously glad to see him.

He was nicely dressed in a great pair of slacks and another gorgeous sweater, this one in navy merino wool. He smelled terrific, as always. It was just the smell of his skin, because there wasn't a cologne that could smell like that. When she came downstairs she thought she was overdressed and was about to change when Todd said no. "Please don't even think about changing," he said fervently. "You look perfect just the way you are. Better than perfect. Don't change a thing, Emmie."

She was wearing a black Herve Leger dress that Sherri had scooped up at a consignment shop. The tags were still on it and everything, and it fit her like a second skin. It had taken three days for her to learn to walk in the heels she was wearing, but the look on Todd's face made it all worth it. "Are you sure I'm not too dressed up?"

"Not for where we're going. You look beautiful, baby."

Lucie and Ayanna just beamed at the two of them. "Have a good time," they said and practically pushed them out the door.

She'd assumed he was going to take her to a

restaurant, but they went back to the loft. It looked even more inviting than the night before because there were more flowers for her and lots of expensive scented candles, too. He led her into the living room and showed her a table set for two.

"Did you cook for me?" she asked with a smile. "That's very sweet, Todd."

"No, I didn't cook this time, but I think you'll like it better. In fact, I know you will. But first, I have to tell you that you are the most incredible woman I've ever known and by far the most beautiful. Happy birthday, Emily."

He put his hands around her waist and kissed her as she wound her arms around his neck. It felt so much like the kiss at the end of a wedding ceremony that she had to blink to keep back a tear.

"Thank you, Todd. You're wonderful, you really are."

"Let's dance," he said.

A look of pure panic crossed her face as his words sank in. "You like to dance?"

"Are you kidding? I love it, come on," he urged. Before she could protest, he changed the music to some old-school R&B and he was leading her in an intricate and sexy dance.

"You're good, baby. You're better than your sister, and I once danced with her in a fundraiser. You have some serious moves on you, woman."

She threw her head back and laughed. "If only

you knew how funny that was, sweetie. If you only knew."

After they danced up an appetite, Todd seated her for dinner. He poured champagne and toasted her with a flourish and went to the kitchen to bring out a serving cart. When he served the food, Emily almost wept.

"Stone crab claws? How did you know they're my favorite?"

"You told me when we were on Hilton Head. We were at that roadhouse, remember?" He smiled at her obvious pleasure. The crab claws were beautiful, already cooked and chilled. They had a unique appearance with their pale beige color and black tips. Emily allowed Todd to drape her with a big napkin to prevent spills.

"I should have changed clothes," she told him. "These look so good. But where did you get them from?"

"Joe's Stone Crab in Florida. They flew them right up, even the key lime pie."

He took a seat across from her. "Todd, don't sit way over there, come sit next to me," Emily said. When he moved, she leaned over and kissed him hard. "This is so special, Todd. You have no idea how much I appreciate you doing this for me. I feel so spoiled," she admitted. "No one has ever treated me like this before."

"I don't see how that's possible, but I'm very

glad I was the first. I'll be happy to spoil you for the rest of your life if you like."

Forcing herself to stay in the moment, she gave him a bright smile and changed the subject. She showed him how to crack the crabs and fed him the first bite dipped in the piquant mustard sauce from Joe's. They ended up feeding each other an inelegant amount of crab, along with coleslaw and Joe's special creamed spinach. The meal was heavenly and they enjoyed every bite. "This was the best birthday ever."

"This was just the beginning, sweetheart. You act like the celebration is over. I'm going to clean this up, and you go get comfortable."

Emily took a few minutes to brush her teeth and wash her hands to banish the scents of lemon juice and mustard from her fingertips before going back to the living room. Todd was waiting for her with a pretty gift bag. Apparently, the sinfully expensive dinner wasn't his only gift to her. As she walked to the sofa, Todd lay back against the pillows and held out his hands, pulling her down on his lap. He kissed her neck and asked, "Are you having a good time?"

She sighed with happiness. "You know I am."

"Good. I have something for you," he said casually, as he reached for the gift bag and took out a small box. He handed it to her and she stared at it for a long moment. "It's not self-opening," he teased.

She tore the paper off and opened the velvet box it contained to find a large pair of thick, heavy yellow gold hoop earrings. This time she couldn't hold back a tear.

"These are so pretty," she whispered.

"You like them?"

"I love them. And I love you," she answered softly.

"I'm glad you like them, because I think these go with the earrings." He handed her another box. This one contained two thick bangle bracelets. They were a perfect match for the earrings, very high quality with a simple elegance that really set them off.

"Are you crying? Don't cry, baby. I thought they kind of looked like you because they weren't real busy with a lot of little doodads on them. If you don't like them, I'll take them back and you can get whatever you want."

"Don't be silly, they're wonderful," she told him. "I don't want anything else. I just want you."

Todd sat up and took her hands. "Me, you've got. Let me show you what I mean."

He stood and very gently pulled her to her feet. In less than a minute they were in the bedroom.

Chapter 17

"You are a work of art," Todd said reverently.

"This dress is the art, dear." She turned slowly so he could appreciate the way the silky black knit shaped itself to her curves.

"Don't be ridiculous. You make the outfit. It's not the other way around." He was sitting on the bed watching her as if every inch of her was precious beyond price. "I want to undress you."

She went to him and turned around so he could pull down the zipper, which he did slowly and carefully. He stood so that he could kiss the nape of her neck then the sensitive spot at the top of her spine, licking her down her back as he gently slid the dress off her body until it puddled on the floor.

She turned to face him so he could undo the tiny front hook of her crimson bra, freeing her round breasts so he could kiss them and squeeze them until they were both aroused and almost ready. She was holding on to his hips while he started taking off her panties, which were the same sultry red as her bra. Once she stepped out of them she was wearing nothing but the black stilettos that took her hours to learn to walk in.

"Now I'm going to take your clothes off," she told Todd.

"Be my guest." He held his arms out while she slowly removed his sweater. It was time-consuming because she was giving his chest the same treatment she'd received, licking his flat nipples and running her hands over his smooth, hard muscles and kissing the fading scar where he'd been attacked in the emergency room. Once the sweater was off, she started on his belt, but the heavy gold buckle slowed her down until she figured out how it worked.

She planned on taking her own sweet time with his pants just to prolong the anticipation, but he couldn't wait. He had the pants off in less than twenty seconds. "It's not my fault that you're this fine, Emmie. We'll work on it for next time."

He picked her up and placed her in the center of the bed, kissing away her laughter. "Don't laugh at me when I'm making love to you, woman."

"Never, ever, ever," she sighed, as he parted her legs and used his tongue and lips to bring her to a place she'd never been before. She was on fire from head to toe, her fingers tearing at the sheets, but he didn't slow down. Every stroke of his tongue made her fly higher and higher until she was screaming his name. He finally relented and moved so that he was holding her tight.

"Hey, baby, I've got you," he whispered.

"I'm yours," she replied.

He turned over so he was on his back, and he lifted her so she was on top of him. "I want to watch you," he said. He thrust upward while holding her hips, smiling at the gasp of surprise from her lips. They began rocking, her hips moving until she was positioned to accommodate his huge, heavy length. He pushed against her, harder and harder, watching her face as her climax began. Her nipples were bigger than he'd ever seen them and he could feel the hot, wet walls squeezing him and releasing, squeezing him again and again until he started to come, too. Her eyes were closed and she bit her lower lip as he kept pumping, holding out for as long as he could. When they were both bathed in sweat and her back arched, she tightened on him again and again until she was in control. He let out a sound from deep inside that was a cry of pure passion as she clenched him so tightly it made him come harder than anything he'd ever experienced.

The tremors didn't stop; they kept on rippling through his body. Emily was still feeling it, too; pulsing and tightening on him with every one. He was still holding her hips and she was still pulling him in, clenching and releasing. Neither one of them wanted to stop. Turning as if they were one person, Todd moved on top, but she was still in control. Her legs locked around his waist and she flexed again. He rose to his knees, holding her hips and her pretty behind. He pushed and she pulled again, and the passion built even higher. When she opened her eyes to look into his, he pushed harder and climaxed again but this time along with her before they fell onto the mattress. He'd never had loving like that before, and he knew without a doubt that he would never have it with anyone else but her. Never, ever.

"I know I promised you a shower, but the bath seemed like a better idea," Todd said.

The huge bathtub, with its air jets to gently bubble the water, had indeed been the perfect place to relax after their wildly passionate lovemaking. Now they were in bed, Emily curled up next to Todd with her head on his chest.

"The bath was perfect. Everything was perfect. You're pretty perfect, as a matter of fact."

"You are so wrong about that I can't even begin to describe it."

"Then don't." She was so tired that she knew she'd be asleep any second. Todd sounded equally spent, but they couldn't seem to stop talking.

"If I was to give you another gift, what would you say?"

That woke her up. Her eyes grew wide and she was about to answer when the sound he couldn't ignore broke the silence. He cursed but answered the phone.

"What? When? Who else? Okay, on my way." He looked disappointed but also calm and alert. She had started thinking of this as his poker face.

"I couldn't say no. They're airlifting victims from a massive pileup. I gotta go, baby."

"I understand, Todd. Completely."

"I'm glad you do," he murmured. "By the way, I'm pretty sure we made a baby tonight." He kissed her hard and laughed gently at the look on her face.

He was gone in minutes and she was suddenly wide-awake.

She was tired, but it was a wonderful, relaxed feeling, even though Todd's warped sense of humor was a bit much. He'd been kidding about making a baby, but it wasn't cute. Well, it was kind of cute, but still... She decided to tidy everything up, starting with the bedroom. When she looked in her roomy leather bag she smiled, because her thoughtful sister had sneaked in a sweater, heavy leggings and a pair of flats. Happy she wouldn't have to put on the dress again, she got to work.

She took the sheets off and laundered them in the kitchen. The place had everything, including a stacked front-loading washer and dryer. Every single thing that was out of place was washed, polished and put away, mostly the dishes from dinner. There wasn't much to do in any part of the loft, really. Emily just polished up everything so it would look pristine when Todd got back. While she was putting the freshly dried sheets on the bed, she turned on the small flat-screen in the bedroom. It was on CNN, and a special report was airing about the horrendous freeway crash that had occurred earlier. This was the reason Todd had to leave, even though he wasn't supposed to be on call.

Emily was engrossed and saddened as she watched the newscast. A semi had crossed a median and crashed into a chartered bus carrying high school students going to perform at a college football game. Several cars were also involved, resulting in five dead on the scene and many more injured. Most of them had been airlifted to Chicago, to Todd's hospital. The news reporter actually said that their chances were measurably better because of the outstanding trauma unit headed by Dr. Todd Wainwright. The footage shown was grim, at best. To see all the flashing lights, bloodstains on the freeway surface and crushed and blackened cars was terrible, just soul-crushing. If it hurt her to look at it, how could he just wade into the middle of it and do what he did? Emily felt humble in the extreme.

She had done triage work after Katrina; she'd been to Haiti and other scenes of disaster, but not as a first responder and certainly not as a surgeon. It was weeks after Katrina and the Haiti floods when she arrived to help out. What she did was act as relief for the doctors and nurses who'd been doing the real work. Looking at the television screen really reminded her of what a difficult career he'd chosen. She was proud of him, but even more displeased with herself.

He'd done everything he could think of to please her on her birthday. He was by far the kindest, most thoughtful man she'd ever known, and he was man enough to admit when he'd made a mistake. He had owned up to everything he'd done wrong in their relationship, and he'd asked for a chance to make it up to her.

But she didn't do the same for him. She hadn't leveled with him; she hadn't shown him any honesty at all. She really was a piece of work, and now she was a sniveling coward, to boot. For someone who never cried, she was sure making up for an arid past with plenty of waterworks.

She couldn't continue to futz around the loft, and she would have felt like the biggest louse in the world if she just kept sitting there blowing her nose. So she did the only thing she could think of. She called a cab and left.

Todd felt at least a year older when he finally left the E.R. He couldn't remember what time he'd gotten there, and he wasn't sure what time it was now. The only thing that registered with him was each patient he had treated. He was still in scrubs; he'd changed them many times that day and gone through a lot of surgical gowns. Normally he changed, but it wasn't on the top of his list right now. He stopped by the main desk before leaving, which was a break in his usual exit trajectory. Normally he went straight out the back. If he had, he would have missed the most welcome sight in the world. Emily was waiting for him, sitting on a bench near the door.

"Emmie, what are you doing here?"

"Waiting for you. Let's go home."

"That sounds wonderful, baby."

Chapter 18

After her day at the hospital, Emily was pretty drained herself. She had introduced herself to the hospital administrator and showed her credentials. "I know I can't do patient care because of the liability, but if there's anything else I can do to help, I'm at your service."

She had kept busy all day, sitting with frantic families and letting them use her cell phone, relaying messages, getting them food or coffee or soda, and doing whatever else would be helpful in a situation like this one. She never mentioned Todd's name, because she wanted to protect his privacy. It wasn't anybody's business why she was in Chicago, so she just kept it quiet. But by the time she got Todd home, in a hot shower and in bed, she was ready to drop. After he was sound asleep, she left for the second time that day, but she did leave him a note.

She was back at Ayanna's house, and while she really wanted to lie down, her mother and sister and even her brother-in-law were cooking. The next day was Thanksgiving and there was a lot of cooking to do, even though they were going to be eating at Nick and Dakota's. She put on jeans and a T-shirt and got to work. Johnny was making rolls, a special recipe which no one could duplicate because he didn't measure anything with utensils. He simply used his hands. They were the best darned rolls anybody ever tasted, and Emily was trying to learn his secret.

Her mother was stirring up a red velvet cake and asked, "Emily, honey, do you want to make a carrot cake?"

"Mommy, you know I need to stay in my lane. I'm still cooking with the decimal system, and that's not on the list. I can make pie. Will that do?"

"Go for it, girl."

For someone who claimed she didn't cook, Emily contributed a lot to the feast. She made sweet potato pies, apple pies, peach cobbler and cranberry-orange relish. She also made two different kinds of potato salad, coleslaw, sweet potato casserole and a very fancy gelatin salad. Emily worked tirelessly and cheerfully, taking dish after dish downstairs to the other kitchen. Ayanna's basement had included a full kitchen, which came in very handy during the holidays or just for any entertaining. But after her tenth or twelfth trip, even a superwoman like Emily got too tired to move. After her last trip to the kitchen she closed the refrigerator and went over to a doublewide chaise longue, where she promptly fell asleep.

The steady hum of people talking was gradually waking her, but she didn't want to give in to consciousness. She willed her eyes to stay closed and focused on a pleasant hum near her cheek.

When Todd woke up, he wasn't pleased to find himself alone in the loft. Even though Emily had left him a loving note, he wasn't satisfied. He got dressed and went to remedy the situation post-haste. Lucie and Ayanna were surprised to see him, but Johnny wasn't.

"Looking for your lady? She's here, somewhere," he drawled.

Lucie looked puzzled for a moment, trying to remember where Emily might be. "She might be downstairs. She was putting things away, I think."

And sure enough there she was sound asleep, showing no signs of waking up. Todd couldn't bear to try, because he knew how tired she was. He sat down on the side of the chaise and stared at her for a long time. He slid in next to her so her head went onto his shoulder, and he kissed her forehead gently. Lucie sat on an adjacent love seat and watched them quietly, until Todd spoke to her.

"I got called in to the E.R. because of that interstate pileup. You heard about it? I was there for about twelve hours, starting at four a.m. And when I got ready to leave, she was waiting for me. Can you believe that?"

"Of course I can, she's my daughter. She's a very giving person, even though she doesn't acknowledge it."

"She was working the whole time she was there, Lucie. She was running here and there and helping anybody who needed anything, and she never told anybody she knew me. I called to check on a patient, and one of the charge nurses told me about it. She saw us leaving together and she figured that we had a relationship, so she filled me in on it. She thought Emily was just amazing. Which she is."

"She is. She's a very unique and special person. I always wished we were closer," Lucie confessed. "We're a lot closer now, but when she was little, she was a daddy's girl, through and through. She was so different from her sisters, and sometimes it made her life difficult."

Todd frowned. "Like how?"

"She was so tall and shapely that people didn't

believe she was mine. Ayanna and I are both small, as was her oldest sister, Attiya, and Emily was tall and athletic. Attiya and Ayanna were known for being good dancers and cheerleaders. When Emily was a baby they dressed her up like a cheerleader and took her to all the games. She was their little mascot," Lucie smiled. "Then she shot up and she was much taller than the other girls her age, taller than everyone in the house except her daddy. People acted like she was a giraffe or something. They just assumed she was clumsy or unfeminine. I once had to cuss out a teacher over my baby girl."

"Go 'head, Lucie. What had she done to Emily?"

"She wouldn't let her try out for the dance team. The heifer told her to her little face that she wasn't suited for it, even though she could dance circles around those children. She didn't even tell me! If her little friends Sherri and Alexis hadn't clued me in, I still wouldn't know."

"That's crazy. First of all that a teacher would be so cruel to a child, and second is the fact that Emily can dance her ass off."

Todd tried to apologize for the slight profanity, but Lucie waved him off. "I said much worse, believe me. It was cruel and it was a lie because she really can dance! Her sisters taught her and she could outdo them in everything by the time she was three. I think the teacher was trying to get next to me because she never got over the crush she had on my husband, the evil heifer. I will never forgive her for hurting my child. Emily was so hurt it was like the straw that broke the camel's back. From then on she was a total tomboy. She didn't think she was pretty enough or feminine enough to be like her sisters, so she stuck to her daddy like glue and learned how to shoot and hunt and gut fish and camp and all those things. I never could get close to her again, not really."

It was plain that the memory still bothered Lucie. "Why do you think that was?" Todd asked with an empathetic expression.

"I'm sure you've heard about the tragedy in our family. My oldest daughter was murdered by her ex-husband, and it just about destroyed us all," Lucie said sadly. "Emily's the youngest by several years, and it hit her so hard. She was so scared and so heartbroken, and I was almost useless. I was helping Ayanna take custody of Attiya's sons, Alex and Cameron, which is what was in her will. Poor Emily just stayed even closer to my husband. And less than two years later, he died suddenly. Well, then Emily just shut herself off. She lived to study and learn and nothing else. She put everything she had into academics. In a way, she's never left school. It's her safety zone, her haven. She's come out of her shell a lot in the past few years, she really has. She's like a different person."

Todd looked thoughtful after Lucie's words. "It's strange, but she's always been the same to me. When I first saw her at Ayanna's wedding, I thought she was adorable because she looked so bored and so damned smart." He pulled out his BlackBerry and scrolled the pictures, holding it out to Lucie. There was a series of pictures of Emily looking bored with her arms crossed, another with her looking downright grumpy and still another with her sitting with Alex and Cameron wearing a genuine smile on her face. "See? I've had those pictures with me ever since. Emily was tall, pretty and had the mind of a rocket scientist. That's my kinda woman."

"I could tell," Lucie said dryly. "I know what a man in love looks like."

He laughed. "See, that's where she gets it from. You're very astute, Lucie."

"And you know this," she said pertly.

"You know I'm going to marry your daughter, don't you?"

"Yes, dear, I do."

"I'm sorry. I don't think I'm supposed to tell you that. I think I'm supposed to ask your permission or something."

Lucie laughed. "Oh, really? You think Emily would appreciate you asking for her hand? I thought you knew her better than that."

"That's true. She'd probably split my skull if

I tried it. I haven't asked her yet, but the ring is burning the proverbial hole in my pocket."

Lucie tried to look innocent as she asked, "Do you have it with you?"

"Nobody sees it before Emily. Nice try, but no sale."

Lucie pouted and snapped her fingers. "Shoot. What a way to treat your future MIL."

"Don't hold it against me, Mom."

The sound of their laughter drew Ayanna to the lower level.

"What's so funny?" After Lucie whispered the answer to her, she started giggling too, and Emily woke up.

She stretched a little and smiled at Todd, then remembered where she was. Her mother was seated on the adjacent love seat and her sister was there, too. Emily looked totally puzzled.

"Did I miss something?"

Chapter 19

No one was surprised when Todd made it clear he wasn't leaving the house without Emily. Ayanna even packed her things in a big leather satchel. Lucie gave her a peck on the cheek and a breezy wave. "See you in the morning, sweetie."

Emily didn't protest his plan, because she wanted to be with him more than anything. She was happy to see the loft again, because it might be the last time. She was trying to be happy and upbeat, but it wasn't easy. She'd been asleep during the bulk of their conversation, but she was almost wide-awake when he started talking to Lucie about marrying her. She had panicked then and she was still as nervous as a cat. Sooner or later he was going to ask her the question that she didn't think she could answer.

To avoid it, she took a long shower by herself. She didn't even have to make an excuse to Todd, since he was busy with something else, thank God. After she showered, she dried her body with half-hearted enjoyment at the pleasurable blow-drying sensation. Wrapped in Todd's navy robe, she was perched on the side of the bed, smoothing body cream into her skin, when the moment she was dreading came. Todd came into the bedroom with a very loving expression on his handsome face.

"I can help you with that," he offered. She scooted back until she was in the center of the bed and he sat across from her so her legs were draped over his lap. He took over the task of rubbing the scented cream into her legs, starting with her feet. He gave a great massage, and he talked to her as he soothed the tension away.

"Emily, when I left Hilton Head and told you we'd made a mistake, that *we* were a mistake, I was trying to explain that I felt bad about the way I'd treated you because I rushed you into bed without getting to know you the way I should have. I hadn't taken the time to take you places, buy you expensive gifts, talk to you for hours on end, rub your feet and cook your dinner, none of those things. I think I fell in love with you the moment I saw you again. Not naked in the shower, although that was nice. I mean when I woke up and you were telling the police I was a sneak thief or whatever. I lost my heart right there and then to your raggedy shorts, the shampoo in your hair and you."

He took a small velvet box out of his pocket and put it in her lap. "I hope you know that when you marry me I will spend the rest of our lives doing all the things I didn't do the first time so that this time it will last forever."

"Todd, I love you so much it makes me crazy. You're the most wonderful man I've ever known. But I can't marry you, not like this."

Todd stopped rubbing her legs and changed position so that he was resting on the pillows at the head of the bed and she was cradled against his chest. He wrapped his arms around her while she dabbed at her eyes with the sleeve of his robe. "Not like what, baby?"

It took her a long time to explain it, but she did her best. "I was mad at you, because you broke my heart. When you said it was a big mistake, it just crushed me, but I wasn't going to admit that to you. So I decided to get a new look and be so sexy and exciting you'd be really dazzled. But you weren't, or at least that's what you said, so I was really pissed. And then I saw you hugged up with some wild woman, kissing her right out in the street after you acted like I was a painted woman, and that's when I decided to get you good."

"A wild woman?"

"Yes, some woman with crotch-high boots and a fur coat and all that stuff. After you had told me I looked cheap or whatever. Who was that woman, anyway?"

"That was my friend Cecily, who had just told me she was moving back to Omaha because she was tired of being a video model. We dated for about three weeks before she decided that her heart and other body parts belonged to the NBA. Okay?"

"Okay," Emily mumbled. "But I didn't know this at the time, so I was still out to get you."

Todd was still completely calm and relaxed. "How were you going to do this, sweetheart?" He brushed her hair out of her eyes and kissed her cheek.

"I was going to be really nice to you and look really sexy so I could seduce you."

"You wanted to seduce me?"

"Yes, of course, but not just that. I wanted to screw your brains out and then drop you like a hot rock right before I went back home."

"That was your plan? Seduce, screw, dump and retreat?"

"Yes, and I know that makes me a terrible, shallow and vindictive cow, and I'm sorry."

"Why are you sorry? It worked."

Emily covered her face with her hands because she didn't want to see the look on his face.

"It worked well, too, all except for the dumping part. That didn't work so well, because I'm crazy about you and you're crazy about me and you're mine for life. And that other part, about going home, well, that's debatable too, because wherever you are is my home and wherever I am is your home. Agreed?"

Emily stared at him intently, putting one hand on each side of his face. "Do you mean it?"

"Look at me, Emily. Can't you see how much I love you?"

"Yes," she said softly.

"Say it louder. Holler like you did the last time we made love," he said with a grin.

"YES!"

"That's more like it. Now look at the ring and let me know if you like it, because your mom is really impatient about seeing it."

It was a wide, thick rounded band of yellow gold with an astonishing stone in the middle. It was big and had an intricate cut, and the colors that shimmered through it defied description.

"I love it. Put it on me, please. What is it?"

"I have it all written down because it's a bunch of things I can't pronounce, and it cost more than my med-school tuition."

"You're crazy. Kiss me, please."

"Sweetheart, whatever you want, whenever and however you want it. For always." He kissed her long and hard. "But I'm also going to make love to you."

"That sounds much better," she agreed. "Since I'm almost naked, it sounds like a really good idea."

Todd had her out of the robe before she could blink, and she helped him out of his clothes just as quickly. Just before he entered her, something crossed her mind. "You were making a bad joke about the baby thing, weren't you?"

He smiled at her in the very intimate way that only she had ever seen. "No, I wasn't kidding in the least."

Chapter 20

"So when do we tell the family?" Todd was sprawled across the bed, watching Emily getting dressed. Thanksgiving morning had dawned bright and cold, and it was time for them to go have breakfast.

She smiled as she pulled a bright blue cowl-necked sweater over her head. "I'm pretty sure it's common knowledge by now. But how about after we make some decisions about where we're gonna live?"

Todd reached for her as she began to put on a pair of jeans, but she slid away. "No! Once you get that look in your eyes, it's all over. Put on a shirt or something so we can talk."

"I just assumed you'd want to stay in South Carolina," Todd said. "I'm sure I can get a job down there with no problem."

Emily zipped up her jeans and sat on the bed again. "Suppose I want to stay here?"

"Here, where? Chicago?" Todd looked dumbfounded.

"I like it up here. I like being around my family and your family. And I think it's time that I cut the umbilical cord at USC. I've been there for far too long, and it's time that I move on and test myself in a new academic environment." She told him about the oddly prophetic conversation she'd had with Dr. Awerbuch before the holiday. "Sometimes you have to make a big change in order to see real progress in your life."

Todd grabbed her, regardless of her admonishment about putting on clothing. "I think we've made a lot of big changes already. What will your mother say if you move?"

Emily laughed. "She'll say welcome to the neighborhood, since she plans to move up here, too."

He laughed, too, and then turned serious. "My career isn't any more important than yours, baby. I don't want you to think that."

"But you're more important to me than my career. I love you, Todd, and I'm not exactly lacking in credentials myself. I can easily find something to do up here."

He kissed her hard and was making another move when Emily remembered to ask about his parents. "Have you told them?"

"It can wait. You've never met them and we should put that off as long as possible. They aren't like Billie's parents, or yours. They're on the snotty side, to be honest. And my sisters, the plastic surgeons, are impossible. Whatever you do, don't believe a word they say, because the truth is like Botox to them. They inject it here and there so they can reshape natural events. And they like to make trouble, so if they tell you my name is Todd, don't believe them."

"That's awful! How can you say things like that about your own family?"

"You'll see. Don't say I didn't warn you. Can I have one more kiss?"

"Maybe just one," she murmured. "Just one little one."

It was quite a while later before they made it back to Ayanna and Johnny's house. No one commented on their long delay in arriving or on their exceptional appetite for breakfast, because they were too busy getting the food loaded into Johnny's SUV and getting the children ready to go to

Nick and Dakota's house. It didn't take very long, and they were soon ready to go. Emily had just picked up Madison when the light struck her hand and the resulting gleam made a rainbow dance across the kitchen. Ayanna was the only one who saw it, and her eyes got huge.

"Don't say anything yet," Emily said urgently. "Just wait until we're all together. Todd and I will spill all, I promise!"

She proved true to her word when, after all the families had gathered and the huge table had been set, Todd asked to say grace, which he did with great dignity and faith. He ended by saying he had a special announcement.

"It will probably come as no surprise that I had the good sense to fall completely in love with Emily and she was kind enough to return the feeling. So we are happy to announce that we will be getting married in the very near future." Emily was seated next to him, and she stood to kiss him and show off her ring.

When the hubbub and congratulations had died down, Lucie posed a practical question. "So when is the very near future?"

Todd and Emily looked at each other with huge smiles. "We were thinking Saturday," she said. "The day after tomorrow, at Ayanna's house," she added.

Everyone started talking at once except Alex and Cameron, who shrugged and started eating. No one noticed Boyd, Johnny and Nick passing folded bills to Jason, who took them with a wicked grin. "I know my brother, and there was no way he was letting her leave here before they made it legal. Pay up, gentlemen."

Todd and Emily were completely serious about a quick, intimate wedding. Neither one of them wanted a big ceremony, although they agreed to a big party in the summer, just to placate the families. They had just the kind of wedding they wanted, performed by Ayanna's minister in front of the big fireplace in her living room. It was just perfect for them, as perfect as they were for each other. Lucie was as happy as she could be, although she warned Emily that there would be bloody retribution when Alexis and Sherri found out what she'd done without them.

"Sherri is in Orlando with Sydney, and I'm sure she doesn't want to wreck her trip. Alexis went to California to visit her sister, and it would be expensive and time-consuming for her to get here in time. And I read somewhere that it's always easier to get forgiveness than permission. Or attendance by best friends, in this situation. They love me. They'll have to forgive me one day," Emily said with a smile.

* * *

Two weeks after Thanksgiving, Emily was making a fresh pot of coffee in her kitchen. Sherri and Alexis were at the door, and she had to hurry to answer it.

"Well, hello, ladies! Are you coming in or are you going to drill a hole in the door with that laser-powered side eye you're giving me?"

"Don't get smart with me. I'll have some coffee, thank you, and a cinnamon roll. I know you made some to bribe us with," Alexis said as she sailed into the kitchen.

"Ditto for me," Sherri added. "And let's not waste any time here. Why are you just coming back to Columbia? You always acted like that university would crumble to the ground if you weren't there to prop it up, so why did you stay in Chicago so long?"

"And why didn't you call anybody or send a text or an email or something?" Alexis asked narrowing her eyes at Emily.

"My, that's a lot to handle at once. Why don't we start with something small? How was your Thanksgiving?" Emily said brightly.

"Fine, how was yours?" Sherri asked as her eyebrow rose slightly.

"It was lovely, thanks." Emily put the creamer and sugar dish on the table, along with a thermal carafe of coffee. Everything else was ready for her friends.

Sherri looked at Emily with new eyes. "Tell me, hon, what happened with that man from Chicago, the one who treated you wrong. Did you see him while you were up there?"

Emily gave her a dazzling smile. "Yes, I did."

Both women leaned forward to get all the details. "So what happened? What did you do? What did he do?"

She hesitated for a moment before holding up her left hand. "We got married."

Before Alexis could scream or Sherri could shriek, Todd came around the corner wearing tight jeans and no shirt. "Baby, have you seen my... Oh, hello, ladies. You must be Alexis and Sherri. I've heard some great things about you, but I think I should get dressed before I socialize." He kissed Emily and waved at the women before leaving.

There was dead silence for a full minute before Alexis said, "Listen, girl, I'ma need to borrow that Hilton Head house for a long weekend. If that's what you come back with, I definitely need to go."

Sherri's eyes were still looking at the spot that Todd had just vacated. Then she looked at Emily, long and hard. "Okay, Miss Girl, you have one minute to come sit your butt down and tell us just what the hell you got into up in Chicago. Don't skip any details, not a one. Starting with that ring," she said with an avid gleam in her eye. "What kind of stone is that?"

Emily sat down and crossed her arms. "It's called a jeremejevite. Isn't it gorgeous?" She spread her fingers to admire it again. "Okay, ladies, here goes. It's not really a long story, but it has an exceptionally good ending. We fell in love, we got married right there because neither one of us wanted to wait, and I'm moving to Chicago because I love it there, my sister is there, my mom wants to move there and I need to cut down on my workload anyway."

"Not the chronic workaholic! Why do you want to slow down?"

Emily smiled into her cup as she thought about the extraordinary passion she shared with Todd the day before he proposed. He had whispered in her ear that they had just made a baby, but it was a few days before she believed him.

Todd came back into the kitchen in search of coffee. Alexis and Sherri insisted that he join them, so he did. Alexis, never shy, asked if he had anything to do with Emily wanting to slow her career down.

"Emily can do anything, we all know that," he said as he covered her hand with his own. "But since this is our first baby…"

"A baby!" they screamed as one. After a few minutes of high-volume joy, Alexis turned to Emily with her hand extended.

"Girl, I'm serious now. Give me the keys to that Hilton Head house, because I plan on spending New Year's there."

Everyone laughed except Alexis, because she meant every single word.

* * * * *

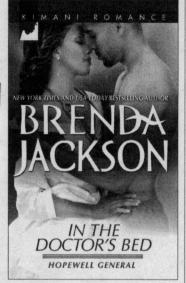

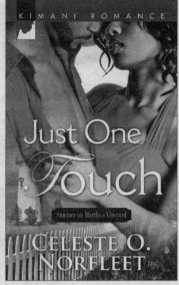

REQUEST YOUR FREE BOOKS!

2 FREE NOVELS
PLUS 2 FREE GIFTS!

KIMANI™
ROMANCE

Love's ultimate destination!

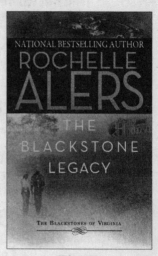